I0591149

More

A Collection of Short Stories

Volume 2

Dr. Dee Hacking

International Bestselling Author and Bestselling Publisher

More

What more do you want than a few haunts, haints, horrors, and mysteries?

Each fright, story, and 2-minute tale here must find the unexpected before **More** begins.

About the Author

Dr. Dee Hacking is a 5x International Bestselling Author, 2x International Bestselling Publisher, Ghostwriter, Doctor, Homeopathic Physician, and Clinician, running her own business for more than 30 years. At her boutique publishing house, House of Wellness Publishing, she is proudly the creator of **The New Rules of Wellness** book series of transformational stories from health experts who lead from the heart, and **SPRUIK IT!: Cultivating the Willingness to Back Yourself to Your Success**, along with fiction and non-fiction, inspirational guided journal puzzle books, and many other projects. Dee hails from metropolitan Melbourne, Australia, and lives in tropical North Queensland with her loving husband, John. Jointly, they are very proud of their three children, young granddaughter, and baby grandson. If you don't find Dee at her favourite coffee hangout or poolside, you will find her curled up in her plush writing nook.

DISCLAIMER

Contents

1. More.

I felt like I wanted to apologise to the people I thought of as old at 50, back when I was a baby of 19!

I was sitting in my usual sunlit café corner of The Bay Bookshop in Sydney, laptop open in front of me, and sipping my usual double-shot latte. I was running multiple internet and social media searches for 'hairstyles for women over 50'. Unfortunately, all I was getting were images of short crops, grey styles, curly bobs...all of which were definitely not ME. I had red hair, courtesy of my Scottish (and Irish) heritage. I had also always felt that long hair was more becoming on me, and didn't see anything to argue with that now that I was 'older', so I would be sticking with my naturally long style.

Tucking a fiery wayward lock behind my ear (no grey yet!), I closed my laptop, and instead opened an old school-shoe box from the 1980s that I had brought with me on my morning walk to the bookstore. I was soon lost in sorting through the contents.

"Whatcha got there today, hun?" asked a well-loved barista.

"Memories!" I replied, giggling, which made me choke on my coffee. "But there is never enough fine brew to accompany such great memories – another, please?"

I picked through the photos, looking for hairstyles from the past. I giggled at my younger self, and I giggled at my schoolmates, none of whom I was still friends with today. Shame.

One photo showed my mother and grandmother, standing at the rear of Grandmother's old farmhouse. Looking at that picture brought back memories of so many warm rhubarb and apple pies eaten, and so many Uno games played. Grandmother's hair was pure white and she always wore it in a bouffant style. She never liked her picture being taken, so in every photo I have of her she's looking down. "Oh, no, not me, Elspeth," she would quietly voice to Mother, with an awkward giggle, when the cameras came out.

The next photo I picked up was taken after Grandmother had passed away. Mother and Father (Elspeth and Peter) were standing in that same spot, but now on the new patio they had built there (they were both very handy and skilled, and looked really proud of themselves), a few years before they had sold Grandmother's farm, when I was in primary school.

Now I was looking at pictures of my various childhood homes in the suburbs. We moved often, so there were lots of pictures. My parents were also crazy about renovating, and made alterations all over our homes. (Sometimes I thought we moved simply so they had new things to build.) There were so many pictures of my parents standing on new decking, walking in a new pool before it was filled with water, posing proudly under their newest gazebo, and starting to plant things in each fancy garden atrium they both built but that Mother always designed all by herself. I shook my head. What WAS their obsession with building structures?

But perhaps they should have put some of that energy into constructing hairstyles – all of the coiffures in these pictures were awful; I could certainly get no inspiration here for today's hair appointment.

I drank the last of my cooling coffee and mused on my parents' continuing structure-creating obsession, which had not waned even as they had aged into being 'elderly'. I made a mental note to tell them not to build anything while I was away this time. I was grateful that they lived next door to me these days – it was good to be able to keep an easy eye on them, while still having my own place to retreat to. But I certainly did NOT need them to have any new renovation ideas while they were doing this latest housesitting favour for me. I also figured that any property purchased from Sotheby's shouldn't need renovating – ever. But if it did? Well, that would be *my* decision.

*****

Much later, back at my said Sotheby's home, I patted my newly pampered head (with some enhancement to the fire in my hair!) as I looked at myself in the antique mirror in my marble foyer hallway. Also in the foyer, in a central pride of place, was Grandmother's huge old grandfather clock. This clock chimed every hour, and I loved it as much as Grandmother once had.

Next to it on the wall was its antithesis – a cuckoo clock left behind by one of my aunts. After Grandmother died, all of the family except my immediate little unit of three had ultimately moved back to various scatterings around Scotland. I had hated the cuckooing of the clock as a child and had detested visiting with that particular aunt and uncle, because of having to hear it. But Grandmother had loved the cuckoo clock too, so for that reason I had agreed to keep it in my house (my parents did not want it anyway), though I had at least muted its undignified cuckooing, so that it was now eternally silent. I was silent, too, as I contemplated the cuckoo clock and thought, as I did every time I stopped here, of my Grandmother's sweet smile. She had been such a happy, gentle soul. She never wanted more than she had; she was such a grateful person and had taught me so much. I was sure I would never get over losing her. It haunted me that her murder had never been solved.

Whenever I thought about someone taking Grandmother away from us like that, I'd get very upset, and very angry – sometimes filled with a seething hatred. But Mother would just say, "Well, Lucy, it's The Noble Truth," as she would play with the heart-shaped locket necklace that always ringed her throat. I honestly began to despise that line – 'The Noble Truth' – referenced like a title every time she said it, as though I was supposed to understand something more behind those simple few words, which I never did.

I had, however, noticed over the years that whenever she began to display any signs of nervousness or irritation, Mother would finger her necklace, then take a deep breath in, and then dress her face with a forced smile – as if this was a purposeful three-step process. But at least she never stayed in a bad mood. Ever. She was ultimately the most relaxed, yet energised, person. I supposed that was a good thing, but I didn't know how much I trusted it, and honestly I found it very difficult to deal with at times.

Mother often had nightmares, too – of little girls in white dresses falling down rung-ladders and dying. Such a strange thing to dream on repeat. When I was little, I'd hear her shouting out after the stroke of midnight, and I would bury my head under my blankets, futilely trying to shut her out. Night after night, especially after she had one wine too many, she would howl and wake herself up, and wake all of us up. SHE gave ME nightmares! Her nocturnal episodes were like something out of a horror movie, with all the screaming and deep growling noises and thrashing around.

Thank heaven for the sunrise! The first light would break, and Mother's demons would disappear. She would be at peace, especially after she took the opportunity to use the breakfast gathering to give me a full rundown of her nightmare. "Oh Lucy," she would say, never missing a morning, "I was trying to save someone, using someone, hitting another person!" I never had any idea of what she was talking about.

I got older, left my parents' home, and made my own way in the world enough to make my fortune…the usual story. My parents got older too, of course, and our relationships changed over the years. I bought my Sotheby's house, and my parents bought the one next door, so now we lived as neighbours. And I knew that these days Mother took a strong antidepressant and no longer had nightmares. I was glad for that, and especially that I no longer had to hear about them! I visited with her most mornings around dawn because we had that in common, that the sunrise was peaceful to us both, and so we often sat together in silence in her kitchen, sipping plunger coffee and watching the golden shine of the first rays of the day.

Aside from the regular morning visits with Mother (and my pilgrimages to the bookstore) I had become something of a recluse. I mostly enjoyed drinking tea, listening to the rain, and, at times, rescuing my cats from their kibble with 'fresh salmon' out of a squeezie packet.

"Moping around," Mother said often, almost as regularly as she had once told me her nightmare stories. (I didn't see it that way.)

If Father was there when she said this, he would defend me: "She's still grieving, Elspeth."

"Seriously, Peter, forever?" Mother usually retorted, sometimes shooting me a look that could freeze the globe – a look that swiftly turned into a broad smile, which I felt was just painted on.

I didn't know how Mother and Father could be so 'happy', and carry on as they always had, with their hectic social lives. When I worked, I had done more than enough hectic socialising myself, both business and personal, to last me a lifetime. I was a wildly successful interior designer, but I had retired the previous year, just after turning 50, and I thought I deserved a little 'reclusive' peace. I was grateful daily too that my short, long-ago marriage had ended without too much fuss. By choice, all I had left of him was his surname, because its rhyme had made for a better business card than my maiden name of Davies. 'Lucy Valentine, Interior Design' had certainly had a ring to it. Silver linings, I told myself.

So now, I was set for life in my 'maybe-a-little-too-fancy-for-me' Sydney seaside home that my parents helped me choose and purchase. Mother had even organised a cleaner for me, though I could have done that for myself, had I wanted to. I actually preferred to do the cleaning myself, but Father said for me not to be ungrateful, and to keep the peace by letting Mother take charge of this one thing. Mother paid for it, so I guessed she had the say, and maybe she just wanted to remind me too that even though I had my own money now, she still had more and it was nothing to her to spend it on keeping someone else's house clean. And indeed she and Father had accrued great wealth over time, somehow. They would never tell me when I was a child just exactly what it was that either of them did for work, and by the time I was an adult I had been cured of wondering – all I knew was that it was something important, with Mother especially dedicating a lot of time to 'honing the investments and looking for prospects'. And at least, for most of my childhood, I had wanted for nothing, other than happiness.

So I thought that I was entitled to be happy, on my own terms, now. I just didn't know if I was sure what my own terms actually were, yet. Something still seemed to be missing. I felt that there had to be something more for me.

*****

Raindrops followed each other, racing down the window to the sill, like a Formula 1 Grand Prix. My eyes always followed the winning droplet, although I still cheered on the wooden-spooner too, always loving the underdog. Even though my 'recluse' life was fairly boring – by choice! – I still looked for enjoyment wherever I could, especially in the rain. I had secretly even considered moving to one of the places supposed to have the rainiest days per year. I could be holed up in a cosy cabin somewhere, but I just couldn't decide which place! Hilo, Hawaii, USA? Babinda, Queensland, Australia? Forks, Washington, USA?

I did feel conflicted, though, and even contradicted – didn't I love my clear sunrises, and my sunlit spot in the bookstore, just as much as I loved the rain? How could I reconcile those opposites? I shook my head. No, retirement hadn't in fact given me what I wanted; being a recluse wasn't quite working for me either. I just seemed to never be satisfied, always wanting MORE…

*****

My little back terrace was divine, and the newest plants I had chosen were beginning to bloom on my sundrenched patio space. I sipped my coffee (because it was coffee for sun, and tea for rain) and admired them.

It was my birthday, again, and I was determined to make the most of this beautiful day, but for a long while I did nothing but sit and dream of a far-off land. I was finally going to be doing something more, having an adventure… I had made a decision, and soon I was heading to the 'Old Country' – Scotland. I felt excitement, and a rise in my blood pressure. Perhaps that was how I knew it was the right thing to do.

I dragged my attention back to the now, and allowed myself to enjoy the idea of an 'escape' from my parents. I had made sure to position myself in the far corner of my patio so Mother wouldn't see me from her kitchen window. They were both glad I was going 'home' to Scotland, but Mother's enthusiasm about it was overwhelming. She and Father had 'upped sticks' suddenly from the UK to Australia, so many moons ago now, dragging Grandmother along too because Grandfather had passed away fairly young. Various other relatives had followed them in quick succession, until a large part of the extended family was here as well. In fact I was the only one of the clan actually born in Australia. And I had never been to the Old Country, even though all of the relatives here had since returned themselves (the last being the aunt who had forgotten to take her awful cuckoo clock with her…) and I could have had a bed with any number of family members in Scotland – if I'd wanted. So I thought

Mother's delight in my trip might even be genuine. I felt fairly kindly towards her at the moment, all things considered.

Mother had insisted on throwing me a combined birthday and farewell dinner, engaging a caterer and getting in a very fancy and very expensive birthday cake, even though 51 was not a special birthday by anyone's reckoning.

"On your birthday, I wish you not just joy and happiness, but also growth and discovery," Mother toasted, raising her sparkling glass high, "for every year is a journey worth celebrating."

I supposed that Mother must have a pleasant heart, even though I had the feeling she was trying just too hard all the time, like it was her 'job' to be happy and positive. She and I did get along, mostly, but there was something that irked me about her, something my father had said I just had to 'learn to live with'. But when I was a child, sometimes he had picked a fight with her in their 'fun way' (as he put it!), and when she left the room in a huff he would congratulate himself and say to me, "It's for us to enjoy the quiet while we can."

Yes, it would be good to get away. I was going to LOVE being away. I was determined to love Scotland.

"You're going to love Scotland!" said Mother, startling me out of my thoughts, too close to almost reading my mind. "Have fun for us, and here is your Aunt Ninny's address for when you get there."

Mother pushed a note in my hand, scratching me with her long painted red nails as she did so, like she used to do when I was a child. And she didn't even notice the blood running down my wrist.

"No need to rush back," she continued. "Stay as long as you like – we will take care of Frangipani and Lotus for you."

I thought of my two beloved feline furbabies, who would hiss and scatter any time Mother set foot inside my front door (I thought they were excellent judges of character). They liked Father much better so I knew they would be fine while I was away, and it amused me to think that

Mother would probably not even actually see them the entire time my parents were on housesitting and petsitting duty.

"I'm sure I will have a great time," I said, smiling and surreptitiously mopping the blood off my hand with the paper containing Aunt Ninny's address. "I will say Hi to everyone for you." I had no intention of staying with ANY family in Scotland. A quick visit maybe, but not staying. My mother didn't need to know that.

*****

A pure white cat dropped from the stone fence to the cobbled road, and I could feel my blood pressure reducing as I watched the majestic feline's fast streak of fluffy white fur elongate itself through the doorway of the tea house. The cat then positioned herself regally in the window and settled down to watching the people. And as I watched her, her demeanour relaxed me. Then she yawned, and stretched sinuously, and came over to my table. She wove her way around my legs, tail held high, and then plonked her warm belly on my toes. She nattered to me, as if we were old friends, and she was telling me a local village tale.

I was sitting and people-watching at the village café, the Garterwood Tea House. Who would have thought that a quaint Scottish village not too far from the Isle of Mull would have such wonderful rich Italian coffee? But the proprietor was an international import, an Italian expat who had been welcomed as a local, with great gratitude. Blairn had once been a busy fishing village, but was now more of a sleepy backwater – albeit with great gelati in summer.

The cat at my feet yodelled up at me.

"Really?" I responded, looking down at her gorgeous snowy glistening coat. I wondered how Frangipani and Lotus were getting on.

"Blizzard is her name," Silvio told me, bringing me another strong cup of coffee. "She showed up here about six years ago – came in as a blizzard was rolling in. First the sea mist came, and then she appeared."

"Who is her owner?" I asked. She seemed well cared-for.

Silvio chuckled and beamed. "Oh, her! She owns herself! She is the village cat; she goes where she pleases, and we all feed her and look out for her. In the winter she chooses someone to hole up with. I'm not sure who had her for her first few winters after she arrived here, but I know that two years ago she was the final comfort of our oldest villager, Mrs Athol (God rest her soul), and last year she was with the MacNeils. We will all be waiting to see who is the lucky one this year, when the first sea mist tells our Blizzard to bunk in for the cold months! I am hoping that someday it will be me she likes for a season."

I thought this was wonderful. "Better than winning the lottery, is it?" I laughed, and bent down to scratch Blizzard's ears.

"Perhaps not quite," replied Silvio, with a wink.

I had been in Blairn just a few days, and was enjoying getting to know Silvio. His café and tea house were also the post office and the general store – the village was that small! He had also made the café part into a summer pizzeria, using his family heritage recipes to make the most of the fresh local produce, and of course there was the amazing gelati. I thought it was no wonder the locals had embraced him as one of their own so thoroughly.

Silvio and his enterprises were clearly a great asset to the village. He was especially proud of himself for reviving tourism and the spirits of the locals, after some 'unpleasant happenings' in the town's past – he refused to give details but he was happy to show off the various certificates of appreciation the locals had bestowed upon him, and which took pride of place on his walls.

"Bella Lucy," he said, "this is a wonderful little village, my true home, and I am so happy to be here."

I hadn't been here anywhere near as long as he had, but I couldn't help it that I was starting to feel quietly at home myself.

The Scottish Highlands were intimately majestic, so stunning and yet unforgiving. Mountains, dales and burns (the delightfully pronounced term for Scottish waterways), and the little villages all connected by single winding roads. Winters could be particularly unforgiving and every member of the little communities would have to rely on each other for pretty much everything. There was clearly a real connection between the people, livestock, pets, and community. I had already been told that spring was a hive of activity, from preparing gardens right through to lambing season. The fields were dotted with Highland cattle, with their stunning long coats with thick fringes covering their eyes. There were deer and goats and geese, too. The purple heather and pink heath and Scottish thistles across the landscape delighted me, superbly idyllic, like I had stepped into a painting. No wonder I was already starting to think that perhaps I would never want to leave.

Blizzard startled me out of my reverie by jumping onto my lap. I welcomed her with gentle strokes along her back, and she purred. Silvio was still standing at the table, smiling at me and at Blizzard.

"I was just wondering how hard it will be to leave here," I laughed.

Silvio laughed too. "It did not take me long to figure out that I was going to stay. We shall see how it turns out for you."

"I came here because my family heritage on my mother's side is originally from this area," I confessed.

"How fascinating!" responded Silvio. "I love that. Any family still here for you to visit, or connections in the area?"

"Not that I know of here exactly, at least not now – there are some MacDougalls still around Perth and thereabouts. And I suppose there must be a bunch of a much older branch over in Cork; so not so very local." I laughed again, and after a pause where he seemed to have to think about that, Silvio joined in too.

"Well," he said, after a little more thought, "some of the older locals might know more about your MacDougall family history here – let me ask around. We can probably come up with something; it's a small place and it gets smaller the more time you spend here."

I smiled and nodded, suspecting that the offer of help was half generosity, and half for some excitement in a small village. "Thank you, that would be wonderful."

"It would be fun for the village to have a little project about our home. Believe me, we all know each other's business!" Silvio half-smiled again, and looked for a long moment at me. And then he continued, in his best forced Scottish accent, "And we all look after each other, no matter what, ma lassie."

*****

Despite Silvio's seeming ubiquitousness, I found that the heart of the Blairn community was really the local pub, one corner down from the Garterwood building. It was actually the only pub in the village, a fact that the proprietor, Paddy (yes, another welcomed expat, this time from across the Irish Sea) said was unusual where he came from – in Ireland, there was a pub on every corner, not just the one.

The pub was simply called 'Paddy's Inn', which made me laugh, and as I sat at the bar and chatted with Paddy, he laughed too.

"She used to be called 'The Welcome Inn'," he said, "but well, she is mine now, and I'm not one to stand on formality!" He grinned at me. "I put a lot of love into her. She used to belong to a gowl and was right banjaxed after he left her abandoned sometime in the 1960s. They were really strange folks, apparently…especially the wee one, a few loose screws, it was said… Anyway, I had a LOT of cleaning up to do!"

As I listened to him I thought to myself, *Lucy, you will really have to learn this Gaelic slang!* But I figured I got enough of the gist of what he was talking about.

"Yes, I basically resurrected her," continued Paddy proudly. "She still needs a lot of work, including my gaff," – he saw me looking puzzled, and quickly clarified for me – "my own living space, at the back; I can't even decide on my favourite colour to paint it!"

I laughed heartily at that. "Well I can sympathise with that problem," I said. "My favourite 'colour' is sunrise, so I'd have a dilemma choosing a single paint, too." I suddenly felt a little bit emotional thinking about sunrises, and I couldn't help wondering about Mother, presumably watching sunrises on her own while I was away. "Sunrise anywhere does it for me…I don't care about the season, or what time it is, either…"

"Oh no," said Paddy, "it will be a miracle if you're up at sunrise here in Blairn, it's not like Australia, you know. And you will be tucked up in your cosy bed if a blizzard hits us in the coming winter!" He emphasised this by pointing towards the outside, before ducking to the end of the bar to serve some other patrons.

"I'm not planning to be here that long," I said, when he returned, as I practically scoffed at the idea of me still being in bed at dawn anyway, "and I never miss a sunrise – it's my special thing."

"Ah, lassie," Paddy shook his head, and pointed to himself, "this place has a habit of keeping people a bit longer than they expect, trust me on that! And you mentioned you had some family in the area long ago? So you have ties to here anyway, whether that makes any difference to you or not."

Paddy handed me a drink in a small tumbler, but I waved my hand in refusal. "I can't mix drinks, one lager is enough."

"It's from the gentleman at the end of the bar. Best take it; can't refuse whisky around here, lass, and the lads aren't usually that generous!" Paddy winked.

I nodded, and turned and mouthed a "Thank you!" to the too-young-for-me-anyway man at the end of the bar, but my lip gesturing was met with a frown.

Paddy pointed to the other end of the bar, a dark corner. *Awkward!* I smiled uncertainly, and saw a hand wave in acknowledgement, and then disappear back into the darkness.

I thought it was a good time to call it a night.

I was back at Paddy's Inn a couple of evenings later. It was a cosy place, probably only holding about 30 people at full capacity. I sat in the well-worn book-nook corner, by the large fireplace. The rest of the room was taken up by a long bar with stools and a few tables dotted around. Paddy had also saved the original kitchen wood stove to give character to the pub space. The actual kitchen area was now new at the back of the building. Paddy had retained much of the original building that contained the four guest rooms, accessed up a set of steep internal winding steps, though he had put in a mostly new owner's residence area for himself (lacking a coat of paint, as I knew) beyond the new kitchen.

I was roused from my doze by a large voice bellowing from that dark corner of the bar: "I hear you are a MacDougall? Silvio tells me you are interested in your heritage – is dat right, lass?"

I blinked and nodded, though I couldn't see who was speaking. I did see that Paddy's head had snapped up at the sound of the large voice, and from behind the bar he looked rapidly from me to the dark corner and back again.

"Come, I've got something to show you!" The large voice had a large owner, and he emerged from the dark corner, almost taking the top of his head off on one of the low ceiling beams. He reached for and rubbed his new cranial gouge. He had masses of ginger locks that fell almost to his waist, and he looked about ten feet tall from where I sat.

"These places aren't made for big Scots!" bellowed the giant, and laughed as he beckoned to me.

I hesitated, and looked at Paddy, who was staring intently at me, before he relaxed and gestured reassuringly that it was safe to go with the giant. I got up slowly. "It's all right, he's MacNeil!" Paddy called to me, as if this would explain everything. I supposed he couldn't have said anything more to me then anyway, over the rising roar of the other patrons all watching the darts tournament unfold on the bar TV.

MacNeil disappeared up the staircase, making sure to duck his head this time. I followed him, not needing to duck. The narrow stairs opened out into a large long passageway, with several old-fashioned windows and recesses and nooks built into it, and a number of doors going off it.

"This will be your room while you're here," MacNeil gestured with one oversized hand to one of the doors, and then continued what was apparently a tour. "This is the shared bathroom, these are the other three guest rooms, and this is what I wanted to show you…"

He knelt and lifted the old tatty carpet right at the end of the passageway, under a window that overlooked the vast walled garden.

"Um, I think you are mistaken…I'm not staying here, I'm at an Airbnb…" I said, finding myself talking to his rear. I noticed a sprinkle of wiry orange hair poking above the waistband of his pants, and looked away quickly.

"Oh yes, you are staying here, when you see this…lookie here, lass…" and he pulled at my clothing. *This is not ideal,* I thought to myself, as I got too close to his armpit and had to hold my breath.

And then I gasped, not from his smell but from what I was now looking at. I ran my fingers along the etchings and scratches on the wall, as MacNeil lifted a loose floorboard, pulled out a hessian bag, and handed it to me.

It took me only a few minutes more to say to him: "Okay, you are right. I'll have my things brought over, and I'll stay here."

*****

The next morning I sat in the Garterwood café with Blizzard on my lap, sipping the foamiest cappuccino, and looking calmer than I felt.

"Well, Silvio," I said, "I'll be staying at Paddy's Inn until further notice. But at least it's closer to here!" I emphasised how good this would be for Blizzard, by scratching her under her chin.

"I thought you would probably end up there," replied Silvio, for no good reason that I could see, but perhaps it was just natural that visitors should gravitate to the heart of the community eventually.

Silvio put a folded piece of paper down on the table. "Bella Lucy, your mama doesn't have email or social media? The post office still has a fax machine, but I was so very surprised to see something come off it last night!"

I shook my head and exclaimed, "Oh, my parents! So many ways to keep in touch, even across the world, and they know HOW to use them, but they just don't!" I wasn't actually annoyed about this – part of having a break from them was being happy knowing that they wouldn't even try to keep casually in touch while I was away. But sending me a fax was a bit worrying – I was immediately concerned for Frangipani and Lotus.

I opened the paper and read it, and read it again. Mother had even worded it like an old-school telegram. I wondered, seriously, if she was actually losing it.

STOP. BUILDING YOU A NEW PATIO. STOP. DON'T COME HOME. STOP. CATS OKAY BUT SENT TO STAY WITH REBECCA. STOP. NINNY HASN'T SEEN YOU SO SHE IS COMING TO YOU. STOP. MOTHER.

Rebecca was one of my interior design collaborators, whose own cat Zinnia was a sibling of Frangipani and Lotus. I trusted her completely with my babies and frankly, would have left them with her from the beginning if Mother hadn't acted so offended by the suggestion of it. Of course, now that it was Mother's idea for Rebecca to look after them, it was perfectly fine… But at least this part was a relief. I was extremely happy to know that Rebecca was taking care of my cats.

I just sighed resignedly about the patio. I couldn't even pretend to feel surprised. That was the Mother I knew well, the inevitable Mother. But it was what I didn't yet know about her that was of more concern to me now.

*****

I sat in the dark corner at Paddy's Inn, where the hairy and stinky informant MacNeil had first sat. I had kept the hessian sack he had found for me yesterday, and I reopened it now and removed its contents. I sprawled the array of documents out in front of me, taking up the entire table space around my lunch plate. There were newspaper clippings, notes written on parchment, pages from a diary, pages of official police reports, and notes of what looked like quotes from a book. I remembered my finger tracing my Mother's name, *Elspeth,* scratched into the wall upstairs, along with an array of dates, like a kind of wall-etched diary. And then the rest... *Holy crap.* It was overwhelming.

"Is this seat taken?" suddenly came a voice from out of a shadow in the dimness, in an unrecognisable thick mixed accent.

I was extremely on edge and easily startled. "Can't you see I'm busy?" I snapped, with more reaction than I would normally allow myself, as I spat out some half-chewed smoked kipper, just managing to catch it with my lip.

The shadow disappeared.

My heart was still racing, but I wasn't sure if it was from the sudden fright or the contents of the hessian sack. The papers in front of me horrified me.

Last night, I had read one of the etchings that ascended the wall upstairs at the end of the passageway: *'Being sent away to New Quay'.* Paddy later told me that New Quay was one of the most remote parts of the UK. MacNeil had added with a bellow, "Should have sent her to Foula!" and Paddy had again had to explain that Foula was a tiny, barely inhabited island in the Shetlands group. But MacNeil's vehemence had rattled me then more than I had realised, so I had left the sack and its contents in my new room at Paddy's Inn, while I organised my full move from the Airbnb to the inn. But now I dreaded that I had no more reasons to avoid facing things and finding some things out.

The newspaper articles were raw and harsh. They detailed how my mother, as a young girl, was caught at school killing animals and leaving their entrails in her teachers' bags. There were other news clippings about missing kids, schoolchildren who had just disappeared. Run away? Scared away? There were insinuations, but no evidence or proof. There were records of how Mother was repeatedly institutionalised and then brought back home, here, to this village, and to this pub, where she was raised. And finally that the MacDougall family had moved her to New Quay, in Wales. Which was apparently where she had met and married my father. And then they must have come back here for Grandmother, and they all emigrated to Australia... So, Mother had run away to the other side of the world to start a new life...

And what, exactly, crucially, might she have been running from?

I didn't know whether to be sick, or to black out, or both.

"Lucy, dear, have you seen a ghost?"

I was startled again, and looked up from the document pile.

"Oh God, Aunt Ninny?" I squeaked. (More than that, it was *cuckoo clock* Aunt Ninny...)

"Oh, I'm so disappointed, Lucy!" Ninny sounded let down. "Why didn't you come to Perth to stay? How did you end up here in Blairn?"

"How did you find me here, Ninny?" I quickly gathered all my cache of paperwork and stuffed it out of view back into the hessian sack. I was doing my best to recover from the shock of Ninny's arrival, on top of everything else, and pretending to be happy to see her.

"I wouldn't miss my Aussie niece's visit! I miss having family around." She smiled a genuine smile, but a sad smile, too.

She sat down next to me at the table.

Now I felt guilty.

I remembered that Uncle Robert, her husband, had passed away several years ago. Mother had only mentioned it casually, and only a few years after it had actually happened, but I still felt thoroughly ashamed that I had forgotten.

"I'm sorry about Uncle Robert, Ninny," I said, taking her hand. "Mother didn't tell me when he passed."

"That's okay, pet," Ninny patted my hand in return. "He was sick, and stressed, and living with a load of guilt, and took his own life…he had a tortured brain."

There was an awkward silence. I didn't know how to break it, much less bring up the contents of the hessian bag I still had hidden under the table, even though I was desperate to get some more answers from family, if I could.

Finally Ninny smiled at me again, sighed, and called out to Paddy to bring her some kippered lunch as well.

And then, amazingly, we sat at the table together for the next hour, and connected as family members in a way we never had when I was younger, back in Australia. Ninny was sweet and gentle, and such a very different person from the Ninny she had been when Mother, Father and Uncle Robert were around her. We even talked about the cuckoo clock, which had been a gift to her from Grandmother. Ninny told me that she hadn't actually liked the cuckoo clock either, and had only kept it around because Grandmother loved it. Ninny even confessed that she had left the cuckoo clock behind in Australia on purpose! I did laugh very much at that, and Ninny in her turn laughed when I told her exactly how I had shut the cuckoo up for good.

"Actually, life is so peaceful now," Ninny said. A tear came to her eye, and she held my hand again. "Is it wrong of me to say that? But there are so many things, Lucy…so many things you need to just put to the back of your mind, and move on…"

But I didn't even know what such things were for me, yet; that was the problem. I tried to bring up darker thoughts of family, but none of my questions led to Ninny revealing too much about anything I wanted to know. I felt her closing down and becoming cagey. All she did was allude to Robert and Mother being 'friends' before Robert began courting Ninny. Ninny had even asked Mother not to talk to Robert alone, once

Robert and Ninny were married. I assumed a love triangle, but Ninny wouldn't elaborate any further.

As if she regretted her lapse into melancholy, and the questions it had triggered from me, Aunt Ninny put on another smile (too close to Mother's kind of fake smile for my liking) and changed the subject to anything and everything innocuous she could think of. I ended up showing her photos of Frangipani and Lotus, received via social media from Rebecca – of course I had checked on my babies immediately (they were thriving with Rebecca and Zinnia). Ninny cooed over their pictures appropriately, we finished with tea and some little cakes, and then Ninny departed to head back to Perth.

I had no energy left for anything else that day.

*****

In the days and weeks following, I was in a kind of limbo. I was both pleased and deflated by Ninny's visit – a contradiction I didn't know how to reconcile. I put the hessian sack back in the cupboard in my room, because I couldn't face its contents, or even think about them and what they might mean. Every day I meant to look at them again, do something about them; but every day I left the sack where it was. One thing I was VERY glad for was the distance between Scotland and Australia, and I figured that it was a good thing to keep for a while yet. I extended my stay at Paddy's, again and again, and floated along – existing, avoiding, even healing. Maybe. I just needed some more time. Just a little more…

The months came and went, and the sea mist rolled in night after night, as winter arrived in Blairn. With the very first sea mist, Blizzard had followed me from the Garterwood to Paddy's Inn, and I knew I was the one to be blessed with her company this winter. It seemed that she had realised before I did that I was going to stay all winter, and maybe even longer. Perhaps she knew that I needed her, as I finally accepted that Lotus and Frangipani, although still beloved to me, had a new perfect life with

Rebecca. I was glad for them, and I was glad for Rebecca, and now I was glad for myself and for Blizzard.

Paddy was delighted to have Blizzard living in the inn with me. He thought that white cats were lucky. Blizzard certainly knew how to make her own luck, at any rate, with another cosy home for the winter. The snowstorms were not far behind the sea mists, and Blizzard snoozed on my bed and kept me company while her weather namesake raged outside. Paddy was proved right, as I was tucked up in bed as the winter sunrises came and went (though I did have an east-facing window!). Every morning, Paddy would personally deliver a tray with hot breakfast tea for me and a bowl of kibble for Blizzard. Sometimes Blizzard ate the kibble, and sometimes she didn't want anything more than all the love and attention I lavished on her.

And I otherwise gave no thought to Australia, and no thought to the hessian bag lost in the bottom of my cupboard.

*****

I felt at home at Paddy's Inn, with Paddy, with Blizzard. More so than I ever had in any of my childhood homes or my Sotheby's house on the other side of the world. I helped Paddy out in the inn now. Sometimes behind the bar, and sometimes with cooking – I even made Australian delicacies like lamingtons, Anzac biscuits, and real Aussie meat pies, and the patrons loved them. Paddy was especially happy that I was also starting to help with the continuing refurbishment of the pub and guest rooms. He was far from finished with his renovations (and I even pointed out a few things he thought he'd finished with, but was clearly mistaken!) and he was delighted with my input. As for me, I felt the vibes and the history and the intrigues and emotions and love from all of the past and present inhabitants of this place. And because the pub was the heart of the community, there was never a dull moment, and I actually revelled in it all. The me who had been an Australian recluse was far from the me who was practically boisterous as an honorary Scot. I could almost describe what I was feeling as 'bliss'. I trusted that I would know what bliss felt like...

My latest project at the inn was to 'spruce up' the book-nook corner of the pub. I was nearly done – I had made new chair pads and cushion covers, and organised new carpet, and done some repainting. And now I was finishing things off by tidying the few old books themselves that lived on the mantelpiece above the fireplace. They were more for looks than for actual reading. Paddy said he didn't think anyone ever read them. I certainly hadn't read any more of them than the titles and authors – because of course I'd had to check that there weren't any valuable antique literary treasures hidden here (nope, just a few odds and ends of volumes the locals had left here over many years). But they were the last part of the book-nook 'renovation', so I reached for them now to throw out any that were falling to pieces, and make sure the survivors would be rearranged in the most artful way on the mantelpiece.

Of course, the first book I picked up did, in fact, fall to pieces as I started to leaf through it. Some of its pages fell loose to the floor, along with a couple of old photographs that had apparently been tucked inside the back cover. I bent and picked up the photo that had fallen face up. It was a picture of a taxidermied squirrel. I laughed, a little uneasily, because I knew this squirrel well.

In all the strange little recessed areas and nooks and crannies along the inn's guest area passageway, various trinkets were housed. Sometimes just more old books, or old candlesticks, or old photographs. There was an old clock and an old nutcracker. They were part of the historic charm of the inn, and the tourists loved them all.

Well, almost all. In one of the bigger recesses there was fitted a square case, with five wooden panels and one glass side facing towards the passageway, so that anyone passing would be able to see the actual stuffed squirrel from the photo on display there. It was definitely the most unusual of the nook objects, and was not always a hit with the guests. But we inn regulars were used to it; we passed it daily without thinking about it or talking about it.

I picked up the second photo, the one that had fallen face down. I turned it and looked at it, and then I recoiled as if I had been punched in the gut, and stumbled backwards. In fact I would have fallen had not one of the pub patrons been conveniently close and caught me before I could hit my head on the mantelpiece or the stone of the fireplace. He lowered me quickly but gently to the floor and yelled to Paddy to bring a dram of whisky. Paddy hurried over with a glass and made me take a big swallow. I breathed deeply, and thought with a fury I didn't know I could generate, *Damn you, Mother!* All of the walling off, not thinking about things, pretending I was nothing more than completely happy and satisfied here, inside and out, had been ripped away by the sight of my mother as a teenager, in that second photo, being the one actually stuffing that squirrel.

I spent the next three days mostly in my room, interacting with nobody but Blizzard and Paddy. I didn't tell Paddy what the actual problem was – he just thought I was recovering from the fright of almost 'tripping' myself into a concussion (or worse). He brought me the daily morning tray of tea and kibble still, and I was soothed by my sunrises and my Blizzard cuddles as I set about rebuilding my mental walls. And I tried not to let thoughts of the abandoned hessian bag in my cupboard come bubbling back to the surface.

*****

Paddy served me the most delicious Irish stew, the first night I came back down to have supper at one of the pub tables. It had rained that day, and it was like magic rain – like it had washed away the recent gloom, and I was feeling good again, and I had a good appetite. I took a large spoonful of my stew.

"How are you feeling?" said a voice suddenly, behind me.

"Dammit!" I squawked, accidentally spitting out a pea onto the table. I glared around at the owner of the voice, as I retrieved the pea and defiantly put it back in my mouth.

"I'm sorry!" he held his hands up in a surrender gesture. "I didn't mean to scare you again."

I realised I owed him an apology, too, along with my gratitude. "It's all right," I said, smiling at him now. "I was able to rescue my pea."

He laughed, and so did I, and I invited him to sit down at my table. He did so, and looked happy to get that far this time.

Since buying me the drink not long after I had arrived in Blairn, and then attempting to meet me properly on the day I had had lunch with Aunt Ninny, he had tried twice more to ask me out, without receiving any assent, enthusiasm or encouragement from me. Not that he didn't seem pleasant, and he was age-appropriate, and he was certainly good-looking, but such things were far from my mind and too complicated as I navigated the progress of the new me in Blairn.

But now I felt that things might be different.

"Thank you," I said sincerely, "thank you so much – I shudder to think how I might have hurt myself if you hadn't caught me. Thank God you happened to be so close."

"You're welcome, of course!" he replied. He got a sort of mischievous grin on his face, which I had to admit I found pretty attractive, and continued, "I didn't just *happen* to be close, though – I was actually just about to ask you out again; see if things had changed…"

"It's possible for things to change," I said, and I couldn't quite believe I was actually flirting, "but I think I would have said No…then."

He was smart; he picked up on that, and looked at me eagerly. "And now?" he questioned.

I smiled widely at him. "Sixth time lucky…"

He stared at me intensely, and it seemed that there was a new spark in his eyes. "Sixth time lucky…" he echoed.

*****

I had fallen in love, and that Christmas was the best Christmas I had ever had. Paddy let me decorate the Christmas tree he put in the book-nook. I had fun buying Christmas gifts for Paddy and Silvio. And also, of course, for Finn. Especially for Finn, because it had been a long time since I'd had someone particularly special to buy for.

He had casually mentioned liking chess, so I had found a beautiful chess set for him, with handmade pieces. He and I had had a romantic Christmas dinner and exchanged gifts. He loved his chess set. Unfortunately, his gift to me had not been quite as successful. He had presented me with a selection of beautiful (and clearly expensive) face-creams and make-up. I appreciated the thought, but also felt guilty, because I didn't put any effort into my skincare routine besides soap, and my days of wearing make-up had ended with my job. I thanked him sincerely but he was too observant not to notice the flicker of disappointment in my eyes, and too smart not to immediately realise what it meant. "I'm sorry, my love," he had said, "it's just that you are so beautiful and I wanted something for you to showcase that beauty." Well, he sure knew how to say the right things!

He wouldn't take the make-up back, saying I might as well keep it in case I decided to try it out in the future – he hinted that maybe there would be 'special occasions' for us down the track where I might like to really doll myself up. And three days later, a new gift had appeared underneath the inn's Christmas tree, with my name written on the large box, and a beautiful (and again, clearly very expensive) maroon-coloured long woollen winter coat packed lovingly inside the box. The coat fitted me perfectly, of course. I genuinely loved it, and Finn was happy to see that I genuinely loved it. And then he taught me how to play chess.

It would have been easy to let myself regret that I hadn't let Finn in earlier, but on the other hand, I also liked to believe that everything ultimately happens the way it is supposed to.

*****

I floated along in the bliss of being busy at the inn and busy at love, studiously ignoring things I still didn't wish to think about. Perhaps if MacNeil had been around he might have pushed me, made me have to face things, but he had left town after his elderly father (known as 'Auld MacNeil') had passed away a month or so before Christmas. Following the funeral, the younger MacNeil had shut up the house that he and his father had shared, and was now traipsing around the Highlands – no one knew exactly where he was, or when or even if he would come back to Blairn. And both Paddy and Silvio, my closest friends in Blairn, who I was sure now knew as much about my MacDougall clan scandals as anyone, refrained from asking questions. I appreciated that.

At first I told Finn nothing of my MacDougall family history, but shortly after New Year's he saw me involuntarily shudder as I walked past the stuffed squirrel in its nook, and questioned why. Before I knew it, it was like a dam had burst, and I was telling him about all of it – my complicated relationship with Mother and the rest of my family; the awful discoveries of my family's past as forced onto me by MacNeil; the horrors I fought as I warred with myself between wanting to know more and wanting to just have a normal life; and the effort I was putting in to try to achieve happiness here in choosing to go down the latter road.

Finn couldn't have been sweeter and more supportive, and it was cathartic for me to express my feelings and receive such support back. He told me he understood a little of my issues. He also had a complicated family history, he said, left behind a little further up in the Highlands. Unlike me, he was actually Scots-born, but had been all over the world (mostly the USA, but a little time even in Australia) after his entire family had left Scotland when he was still a child. He had only returned to Scotland himself just before I had arrived in Blairn. I couldn't believe how well he understood me.

I was sincere when I told him that it seemed like he was an angel from the stars, sent to help me.

He had replied, just as sincerely, "I'll be your angel, if you'll be mine."
I guess we both knew we were in deep.

*****

Paddy was pleased to see me with Finn, too. He correctly figured that it was just one more compelling reason for me to stay in Scotland. He made tentative noises about remodelling the large walled garden area of the inn (he had long ago tidied and planted some of it for the pub's kitchen produce, but a much larger part of it was still disused and overgrown), and was happy to get an enthusiastic reaction from me. I missed my Sotheby's house garden and plants, and I did wonder sometimes if my parents were looking after them. I hadn't heard from my parents for months, and I liked it that way. I certainly didn't want to open a can of worms by initiating contact. And I definitely didn't want to know about new patios or greenhouses or pools or whatever else Mother might have taken it into her head to build on my property. I accepted that I would just be happy to love new plants, Scottish plants, instead. So I assured Paddy that I would stay for several more months; at the very least, all the way through spring.

And then Paddy added, casually, "Well then, perhaps we might even do something with the attic."

"WHAT ATTIC?" I exclaimed. This was news to me!

"You know that tiny storage room off the passageway, next to the fourth guest room?" Paddy asked.

I did know that room. It was next to useless, as most of its space was filled by a heavy old-fashioned wardrobe that took up the entirety of the back wall. The wardrobe held the inn's spare linen and towels.

"The door to the attic stairs is behind the wardrobe," said Paddy. "It's actually quite a large attic, but almost empty now – I took out most of the things that were still useful and usable before we blocked off the door with the wardrobe. Nothing of interest left in it, except perhaps in one of the cupboards up there, but I can't say for sure, because the key to that cupboard is lost." He grinned, and added, "When we do get around to doing the attic renovation, we'll probably have to take an axe to that cupboard door – it's very solid. We can draw straws for who gets the privilege! But that's still a fair wee while off, anyway – ma garden comes first!"

*****

Paddy's garden renovation aspirations were lofty, but they had to take a back seat to the weather. All of January and into February, snow or just too much of winter meant our garden progress was very slow, and what refurbishment work we did achieve was chiefly concentrated on the inside. Finn had proven to be a bit of a handyman too, and I enjoyed working with him.

Valentine's Day came. Finn joked that it was my own special day, both by love and by name. To my surprise and pleasure, he went all-out for me with a dinner he cooked himself (using Paddy's kitchen), that we ate together in my room at the inn, which he had filled with dozens of roses. Blizzard had even discreetly made herself scarce.

"Lucy," said Finn, taking my hand, "I feel like a new man, and that my life has taken on a special meaning." He looked deep into my eyes, into my soul.

I had similar thoughts. "You've made such a difference in my life, too," I responded. "You, and this place."

He got that mischievous grin on his face again, the one that always made me catch my breath a little.

"It feels like home, doesn't it? Our home, together? So, how would you like to be a proper Scot, in Scotland? Get rid of 'Valentine' and bring a Highland name to the fore again…say, 'MacKinnon'?"

I looked sharply at him, gauging how serious he was, but he WAS serious, and he pulled out a ring box and opened it, showing me the most beautiful diamond ring, and before I knew it I was nodding and smiling and crying and saying Yes and getting that ring securely on my finger.

The next morning, Paddy congratulated me as he brought my breakfast tray of tea and kibble. Blizzard had accompanied Paddy inside, and she jumped up onto the bed with a satisfied chirp.

"I haven't even told anyone yet!" I exclaimed.

"Finn has," said Paddy, winking. "I think he wanted the whole village to know, immediately. That's a fine feller you've caught yourself."

I thought so too!

"He asked me for a favour for you, Lucy," continued Paddy, as he left the room. "Come out to the passageway when you're ready."

I dressed and did so.

Paddy was waiting in the passageway, by the nook that held the display case containing the stuffed squirrel – that I avoided looking at, every time I passed it. He had some tools in his hands.

"Finn says this squirrel creeps you out," said Paddy, "so the squirrel has to go! I definitely understand why. But you should have said something earlier, lassie. I forgot the beggar was here."

In spite of my unease at the focus on the squirrel, I couldn't help but laugh at this last bit. "Paddy, you walk right by it every day!"

Paddy grinned and shrugged, and took up the tools.

It didn't take him long to free the case; it wasn't very securely glued into the nook. As he took it out, I saw written on the back of it, on one of the wooden panels that had been hidden from view in its display position: *My best and only friend, Mr Cheeks, May 1961.* I recognised my mother's handwriting; it had not changed in all these decades. I thought I might be feeling sick.

But I didn't have time to be sick, because Paddy exclaimed, "What's this?" as he reached into the nook. There was a small space between where the back of the case had been and where the back of the nook was – enough room to hold a tiny cloth bag, that must have been there ever since the squirrel was placed in the nook.

Paddy opened the bag and shook a number of small grey objects into the palm of his hand. We both realised at the same time that they were children's teeth, about a dozen of them, and Paddy involuntarily snatched back his hand and spilled the teeth to the floor. I was frozen. Paddy recovered and picked up the teeth quickly, putting them in his pockets, muttering something about the Tooth Fairy missing out. Good for him, but I didn't want to think about those teeth at all. I shook myself and picked up the little bag, which had also fallen to the floor, to give it back to Paddy. It felt hard where I was holding it.

"There's something else in there," I said to Paddy. He met my eyes, and took the little bag from my fingers, and very slowly reached into it, and withdrew...a key.

Realisation came to Paddy in a flash. "It must be the key to that cupboard in the attic! There'll be no axe-wielding for us after all!" He saw that I was still pale. "Don't you worry, lassie," he continued. "You won't need to see these things you don't want to see, anymore. You go back in your room, and cuddle Blizzard, and when you feel up to it, come downstairs and we'll all drink a toast to you and Finn!"

That evening the pub at Paddy's Inn was the merriest place in Blairn. Everyone celebrated hard and there would doubtless be some sore heads in the morning. I drank as heartily as anyone – partly to celebrate, and partly, perhaps, to forget.

Finn came upstairs with me to my room.

Once we were safely alone, all he had to do was look at me, and I burst into tears.

"I can't go on like this," I cried. "I don't know what to do!"

Finn held me tight. "You have ME now," he said, "and I'm going to look after you. You've been bottling everything up for so long; I think it's time to try facing it, getting to the bottom of it, dealing with it. I'm here, I'll help you, I'LL BE THERE FOR YOU. Lean on me."

I knew he was right. I felt lighter. "You're my angel," I said.

"No, you're mine," he grinned.

It was our very own private joke.

Things seemed to accelerate after that.

The first thing was that Finn moved into Paddy's Inn, into my room, with me. He was only renting the cottage he had been living in since he had come back to Scotland, and I felt so at home in the inn now, that it made sense he would be the one to move. After we were married would be plenty of time to find our own proper place. The new living arrangement worked beautifully, with the only disadvantage seeming to be to Blizzard, who now had less space on the bed, but she didn't appear to mind.

The second thing was that Finn convinced me to contact my parents, after all these months, to tell them that I was engaged and that I was going to stay in Scotland. And this led to the third thing, which was extremely frustrating – I couldn't get hold of my parents. I supposed it was karmic payback in a way. All these months I had been happy not to hear from them, but now that I was the one wanting to get in touch, they should be waiting on my call, dammit! After futilely exhausting all the direct contact options I had for them, I resorted to asking Rebecca to please go over to the house and tell them in person that I wanted to talk to them. Rebecca reported back that there was no one home, and indeed the house looked shut up and the garden was overgrown in some parts and dead in others. She didn't say anything about the state of my own home (or what new construction might be there), and I was glad, because I didn't want to know, and I didn't ask. One thing was for sure though – I was even more grateful that Lotus and Frangipani were safe with Rebecca. But how typical of my parents to just up and go somewhere and not tell anybody, and not worry about their so-called promises and responsibilities to other people.

I wished more than ever to wash my hands of my parents.
I was going to exorcise them, one way or the other.

*****

"Good morning, today's the day!" said Paddy, greeting me as I came into the bar. Paddy no longer delivered my morning tray to me. Finn did that now, getting up while I still slept, going downstairs to collect the tray from where Paddy had prepared it (with two cups of tea, now), and then waking me gently so we could watch the sunrise together.

"Finn's already emptying the wardrobe," I said, grinning. "He wants to see this attic, see how much extra work we might have to do. Now that we're starting to make some proper progress on the garden, I think he might be worried about major internal renovation distractions!"

Paddy and I went upstairs, and now that the wardrobe from the storeroom was empty, it was fairly easy for the two men to move it out of the room (to where it took up a lot of space in the passageway) so that we could access the door to the attic steps.

The three of us went up into the attic. It was quite gloomy because its few windows were shuttered, but I could tell that it was much bigger than I had been imagining.

"I told you," said Paddy. "A lot of space. Could almost make an extra guest room…"

Also, as Paddy had said, the attic was mostly empty; just some useless odds and ends he'd left behind the last time he was in it. A ladder with a broken rung, a few broken plates and cups, some tarnished silverware, and a few old books. I recognised a very thin volume as 'The Tell-Tale Heart' by Edgar Allan Poe; that one always gave me the chills. Worse though was a title I had never seen before – 'The Art of Embalming' – and I didn't want to think about who might have liked that book.

"This cupboard's the locked one," said Paddy. "The key fits!"

My pulse was racing now.

Paddy swung open the cupboard door.

At first we thought that the cupboard was empty. Then we saw a small pinewood box, nearly the colour of the cupboard floor. My imagination was running away with me now – I could almost hear the box beating, like the guilt under the floorboards in 'The Tell-Tale Heart'.

Paddy tentatively opened the box.

The three of us exhaled in relief. The box held a pair of Dutch clogs, sized for a child. We looked around at each other and laughed and laughed until we cried.

Paddy lifted the clogs out of the box and looked at them. They each had the name 'van Leeuwen' written on their sides. "These must belong to Auld Betje!" he said.

That meant nothing to me, or to Finn either.

"Betje van Leeuwen is one of our elderly villagers," Paddy explained. "Originally from Amsterdam, but been here most of her life. I admit I don't know much about her because she keeps to herself – never seen her come to the pub! Who knows how her clogs came to be here?"

I felt compelled to return the clogs to Betje. "I'll go see her, and take these shoes back to her," I said. Paddy put the clogs back in the box and then handed the box to me.

Finn said he'd come with me, but I shook my head – I felt I wanted to go alone. "Besides," I said to him, "I know you and Paddy are dying to finally dig up the south end of the garden now that the weather is good enough for it!"

Back in my room I changed into nicer clothes and phoned Silvio to get Betje van Leeuwen's address and directions to it. Blizzard watched me from the comfort of the bed.

I picked up the clogs to look at them in the better light of my room, and that was when I realised there was something else in the box – an old photograph, face down. I had a sense of foreboding as I picked the photo up and turned it over.

The picture showed two identical little girls in two identical little white dresses. Faded writing at the bottom of the picture said: *Elspeth and Neve, 1953.*

"Who the hell is Neve?" I shrieked out loud. Blizzard hissed and fattened her tail. I stroked her to calm her down, and to calm myself down too, in all honesty.

I was more tired of all this mystery and misery than I wanted to admit. Time to get some answers, get some *closure,* get some relief so that I could restart my life.

Next stop, Auld Betje.

I took one more thing with me when I left my room – the hessian bag from the bottom of my cupboard.

*****

My knock at Betje van Leeuwen's door was answered by a young woman in a nurse's uniform, who told me her name was Rissa. "Betje is confined to her bed today," said Rissa. "I'll let her know you're here, and make sure she's up to seeing you."

I waited in the entry hall, and after a few minutes Rissa came back and told me I could visit a while. Rissa showed me into the bedroom, where an ancient-looking woman with snowy wispy hair and bright eyes was sitting up in the bed. I sat down on the chair next to the bed.

"Shall I bring some tea?" asked Rissa.

"Whisky!" ordered Auld Betje, staring hard at me.

We didn't speak to each other all during Rissa delivering the whisky and leaving the room again. Nor when I took the box out of my bag, opened it, and handed Betje the clogs and the photograph. She put the clogs down gently, and then looked for a while at the photo, and then sighed.

"I was wondering when you would come to see me," Betje started. "You took longer than I thought you would." She had lost her Dutch accent.

"So you know who I am? Whose daughter I am?" I asked.

"Oh, yes," she said.

"Who is Neve?" I asked.

"Oh, my dear," she replied after a while, and after staring at me with what I suspect was pity, "Neve was your mother's identical twin sister."

Of course I had known this must be the case, from the photograph, but hearing it made it *true,* and Betje's use of the past tense made it *sad.* I took a big gulp of my whisky and braced myself for the details.

Betje explained that her daughter, Cornelia, and my mother had been best friends as children. Mother and her sister Neve and Cornelia had been inseparable. The three were always together, whether at Betje's house or at the twins' home, The Welcome Inn.

"The three of them dressed the same as much as possible," said Betje, fondly remembering. "They liked to pretend they were all sisters."

"What happened to Neve? Did she die?" I asked.

"She disappeared," said Betje. "Elspeth said she got out of bed very early one morning and left the inn. No one saw her again after that."

I thought of the old newspaper articles about missing children that I had in the hessian sack in my bag. I couldn't recall if a 'Neve MacDougall' had been mentioned, but surely I would have noticed?

Betje was continuing: "The day before Neve disappeared, the three of them were at The Welcome Inn to play. They had made a little playhouse space for themselves in the attic – I suppose you would call it a cubby – and they used to spend a lot of time there, and even had meals there. Well, Cornelia came running home to me in the evening, very upset, and covered in blood, saying they all fell from the attic. They had locked themselves in somehow and tried to climb out of an attic window and down the ladder that the gardener had put against the wall to help him reach the ivy he was cleaning up. Cornelia said the ladder gave way and they all had to jump down. Cornelia was very frightened and had a bloody nose but was otherwise all right. And then Cornelia and I went over in the morning to see if the twins were all right, and found out that Neve had gone missing. The whole experience rocked Cornelia and Elspeth to the core – neither of them were ever the same again. It was like one day their world was brilliant, and the next it was dead silent, and it stayed that way for years. We had to separate Elspeth and Cornelia in the end; it was like each was keeping the other down, and the bad feelings around Neve's loss could not be forgotten while the girls were here where it happened. So your grandparents sent Elspeth to a special college in Wales, and I sent Cornelia to my family back in Amsterdam. She lives there still, and she has found peace now. Every year I think about going back to Amsterdam myself, but something keeps me here – maybe I am too old to change. But Cornelia visits me every few years, and she is always sending me things she thinks I will like. Or that she thinks will help or comfort me, like this book…"

Betje held up a book with an orange cover, that I had noticed half-buried in the bedclothes when I first came into the room. I stared without seeing, at first, because I was still coming to terms with the fact that Mother had a lost sister that she had never mentioned; ditto for Aunt Ninny, and Grandmother had never mentioned her lost third daughter – what the hell was WRONG with my family, seriously?

And then I focussed, and read the title of the book Betje was holding, and I gasped. The book was called 'On the Four Noble Truths', and I was instantly hearing Mother's voice, stating over and over, "It's The Noble Truth. It's The Noble Truth."

"Betje, what are The Four Noble Truths?" I asked, almost desperately.

She didn't waste time asking why I seemed to care so much; instead she said, "They are principles of Buddhism. It can be quite complicated, for a beginner. But at the simplest level, The Four Noble Truths relate to dealing with pain. First is on *the acknowledgement of pain,* second is on *the origin of pain,* third is on *the cessation of pain,* and fourth is on *the path to the cessation of pain.* Cornelia could explain it much better than I can – I'm still learning, but she has been a practising Buddhist for many years now. Actually she and Elspeth both became interested, just a little while before we separated them. I have often wondered whether Elspeth continued with it, too?"

I was shaking my head, mostly trying to reconcile why Mother had felt the need to philosophise cryptically about 'pain' to me whenever I had expressed sadness over losing Grandmother. But Betje took this as me confirming that Buddhism had not been taken up by my mother as it had been by Cornelia.

"Never mind," Betje said softly, suddenly seeming very old and tired. She looked sadly at my photo of the twins again. "Reach into that drawer behind you, will you? Please hand me the photo album there."

I did as she asked, and the frail hands turned the album's pages to the one she wanted. She rotated the album for proper viewing for me, and then pointed to an old photo of three girls, a little older than the ones in my photograph. Two were identical, but all three were dressed the same. I studied the photo, and I noticed that all three girls were wearing necklaces. Cornelia had on a choker-style chain, while the twins were wearing locket-type necklaces. And here was the only point of difference between the two identical girls – one had on a star-shaped locket, and the other had on a heart-shaped locket. Of course I recognised the heart-shaped one, instantly.

"Mother still has her locket," I said, and I was unexpectedly teary.

"Yes," said Betje, "they always wore them – it was often the only way we could tell the twins apart. Their parents gave them a locket each. Your grandfather gave Elspeth her locket because he said she was his shining star. And your grandmother gave Neve her locket because she said she was her princess of hearts."

*****

I had left Betje's house with almost rude haste, quickly thanking her for her time, and saying that I suddenly wasn't feeling very well. And it wasn't completely a lie; I felt like I wanted to throw up. I had no more thoughts of discussing any of the contents of the hessian bag with Betje. Or with anyone else. I just wanted to get home to Finn, and feel loved, and protected, and safe.

I arrived back at the inn, went around to the walled garden where I expected to find Finn and Paddy digging, and walked into a scene of absolute chaos.

Finn, Paddy, and two policemen were standing around a dirt-covered long pinewood box, looking down at it and talking excitedly. The expression on Finn's face when he lifted his head shocked me; he looked both haunted and apprehensive. As I watched, he noticed me, and his face changed to a look of alarm. I rushed over to him. He tried to stop me looking down into the open pine box, which I had subconsciously sensed was a makeshift coffin, but it was too late. I could clearly see the skeletal remains of a child, covered in the rags of what had once been a dress. Her skull was caved in on one side. A star-shaped locket necklace was tangled in amongst the neck bones.

Once again, Finn caught me as I fell, this time into unconsciousness.

*****

I had not gone to hospital, but the police doctor had given me a sedative, and I slept a drugged sleep all night. Blizzard was curled up beside me, while the police specialists did their work in the garden, and Finn and Paddy answered questions non-stop. It was mid-morning before I was well enough to speak to the policemen myself.

It was plain enough what had happened while I was out the day before. Finn and Paddy, digging in the garden, had uncovered the coffin, opened it, and Paddy had called the police.

The thing I did not yet know was why the police had arrived at the inn before their station had notified them about Paddy's call.

Finn came to sit with me once the policemen were given the go-ahead to talk to me. I still felt a little ill, but Finn's reassuring presence gave me strength enough.

Or so I thought.

The shocks kept coming.

The policemen had come to the inn yesterday looking for ME. Of course they were then delayed in speaking to me, because of the combination of the garden discovery and my indisposing myself.

I listened numbly as the Scottish policemen explained that they had been contacted by the Australian police, who had requested them to speak to me, before things got into the Australian press.

The Scottish policemen informed me that my Sotheby's home in Sydney was now a crime scene. Human remains had been discovered under my new patio. And under my parents' own patio, so their home was also a crime scene. My parents' location was unknown. The policemen hastened to assure me that I was NOT a suspect in any crime. Of course I knew who the suspects actually were, before the policemen spelled it out for me. They confirmed that the Australian police were right now digging around the clock under the various home-made structures at my string of childhood homes. I accepted that they would find things.

The only time during the whole ordeal that I actually reacted was when one of the policemen said, "And in light of everything, the cold case of your grandmother's murder has been reopened, too." At that, I started to sob.

Paddy had made some cock-a-leekie soup, and I managed to choke some down, at Finn's coaxing. The two policemen, considering themselves off-duty for lunch, sat at the pub table with us and enjoyed some soup themselves. They were otherwise solicitous of me, and talked of trivial things with Paddy, because of course they all knew each other from way back – that was the small village at work again. I felt a little better, and was happy with Finn's suggestion to get some fresh air as he and I walked the two policemen outside to their car. Blizzard even came with us.

When your life feels surreal, apparently there is always room for more madness. A woman was standing by the police car. Waiting. For whom? I wasn't even surprised, at this point. Blizzard arched her back, hissed, and disappeared back into the pub.

"Hello, Mother," I said, too calmly. "Where is Father?"

"Hi honey, I'm home!" Mother giggled. "And your father is back in Sydney, of course, with all the others…"

There she was cut off, because the policemen had sprung into action and grabbed her.

But she had said all she needed to say.

*****

It was late October, meaning that the sea mists could start rolling in any day. Now I was 52, and newly married to my second husband, and living back at Paddy's Inn, after an absence of over eight months from Scotland. From Blairn. From where I felt safe.

After my mother was arrested and extradited back to Australia, I had followed with Finn. I was soon formally cleared of any knowledge of or involvement in the heinous actions of my parents. My father's remains were located, under 'my' new patio, and removed and reburied. I didn't attend the funeral. Finn and I were stuck, though – I was to testify at Mother's Australian trial, and there was all manner of legal untangling and settling to do. Things became somewhat easier on us when Mother killed herself before her trial date was even set. I didn't mourn her or attend her funeral, either; she was already dead and buried to me long ago. Finn and I left Australia as soon as we could, which was still not soon enough. The publicity of the 'Sotheby's Dozen Serial Killer' (SUCH an unfortunate label) was intense enough that we toured discreetly around Europe for a few months until we became old news, and could go back to Scotland in relative peace. I found the travelling quite exhausting, though Finn looked after me well, but accepted it as a necessary evil. I did see plenty of sunrises, though, and shared them all with Finn. He was helping me so much with wiping out memories of a past I needed to forget.

I sat peacefully at the table in Silvio's café at the Garterwood. Silvio had welcomed me back like a long-lost friend; I was flattered. I even flirted a little, while flashing my new wedding ring at him. It was the first thing Finn and I had done when we had landed back in Scotland, staying in Glasgow until we could be married there. We had made a real occasion of it, albeit a private one – I had bought a very expensive dress, and had even deigned to use a little of the make-up that Finn had gifted me the prior Christmas (his eyes sparkled when he saw how I looked all 'dolled up'). We had then headed back up to Blairn for our, as Finn put it, 'never-ending honeymoon'. But as it turned out, we had settled back into our Blairn life more like an old married couple than a pair of newlyweds. And I actually liked that just fine.

Silvio brought me a fresh coffee. "So glad to have you back, bella Lucy," he said again.

"So good to be back, Silvio," I smiled at him.

"And look who it is!" he said, pointing to the doorway. It was Blizzard, of course, and she came unerringly to my feet, plonked herself down on them, and purred up at me.

"Looks like the village has been looking after her well!" I said, stroking her fur, as snowy white as ever.

"Indeed, she is as fat as a meatball, all ready for the winter!" laughed Silvio. "Perhaps this year I will be the lucky one to be blessed with her company."

*****

Later on, I happened to be at Silvio's again, with Blizzard, when the first sea mist rolled in. To Silvio's disappointment, Blizzard leapt off my lap and headed out the door. I had to follow her.

She made a beeline for Betje's house, and I saw Rissa letting her in at a window.

I was glad Betje had been left out of all the fuss. As far as everyone was concerned, I had dropped off the clogs to her, and that was the end of it. I had told no one else, not even Finn, about the photo that had also been in the box with the clogs. I hadn't told Finn about the mystery of the lockets, either – was Betje's elderly mind misremembering, or had there been a locket swap, or had there been a *name* swap? I didn't know, and I didn't want to know. It was all done, and buried, and *in the past*. I was nobody's daughter anymore; it didn't matter whose daughter I had been, nor what my mother had or hadn't done. I was my own self, and I was going to be free.

"My favourite colour is sunrise," I said to Finn, as he and I enjoyed a particularly beautiful winter dawn, and I drank the tea that Finn still lovingly fetched up every morning for me. He had switched to coffee lately, saying that he needed the extra energy for our own renovations, now that Paddy had agreed to us combining two of the guest rooms into a suite for ourselves.

"I think I've heard that somewhere before," he grinned in response.

"Well, I say it almost every day!" I giggled. "Sometimes I think there won't be another sunrise, so I always have to express my appreciation when there is. It's hard to imagine, but one day the sunrises will be done…"

"Every day is a sunrise, with you," said Finn, stroking my head.

"Are you sure you like it?" I asked, flicking my new short bob hairstyle behind my ears. "I guess I had to accept that one day I would be too old for such long hair, and it's a little thinner now, so it actually wasn't hard to let Carole talk me into having her cut it."

"I love it!" Finn reassured me immediately. "It's a new you, and just right for a new us, and our new life."

I snuggled up to Finn, feeling dozy. "Oh, I'm lazy again today, but I really do want to help you with our suite-work."

"You're an angel, my angel, but I'm happy to manage for myself today. You just go back to sleep," Finn kissed me and tucked the blankets around me, "and I'll take care of everything."

I settled back in the bed, as he exited the room, shutting the door quietly. My eyelids drooped, and I sighed, and felt peaceful, and happy. And that finally, I couldn't want for anything more.

2. Snake Tavern.

Gideon watched the condensation droplets run down his pint glass as he sat over his beer. The water vapour moved faster than the drink. He circled the glass on the bartop.

"What's the problem today, Gideon?" the new barman asked.

"Hmph," Gideon let out, without concern. "I just feel there is trouble coming." His eyes flashed up to the barman's smile. "Sorry, what did you say your name was?"

"Gilbert," replied the barman, while wearing a friendly expression, no doubt anticipating that a new guy could get some backlash from the locals, "and yes, I'm new, just up from The Surface."

*****

Snake Tavern, or just 'The Snake', was THE place to be.

Wi-Fi vanished as soon as you entered The Snake, but who needed it, when the beer flowed freely and so did the conversation? There were familiar faces everywhere. This was where mates met, and all sense of time and any responsibilities were left behind at the door.

The Snake was just down from an artisanal patisserie that doubled as an ice-creamery, and which was THE place to be for the ladies. Therefore, all the fellas rated The Snake 100/100 for convenience, especially when the partner called and there was no reception.

At The Snake, there was zero idea of ANY outside needs. The Snake was ultra-convenient – it was a hiding place, like a den.

"Meet you at The Snake?" one pal would say to another.

"Yup, sure will, it's darts tonight, and there has been a change in the tournament schedule!"

*****

Gideon asked Gilbert for the time, because it was hard to tell how time flew by at The Snake.

"It's 3.33 am, Gideon."

"WHAT, oh-three-thirty-three?" Gideon's eyes flashed wide open. "No, you're shitting me? I'll be killed by the missus!"

Everyone laughed in unison.

"It's okay, bro, we will all still be here tomorrow even if you ain't!" one familiar voice shouted out.

"So, is it free drinks when Gid leaves us now?" another joker called from the pinball machine's corner.

"Oh fuck off!" Gideon grinned. "I'll stay for freebies!" He reclaimed his seat, banging his empty glass on the bar.

Gilbert approached. "Who's shouting then, you smart-arses?"

*****

"How was your day, babe?" Lea greeted Gideon at their home of Lower Level 4 Unit #19 after her work day. She wasn't smiling.

"How was *your* day, BABE?" he blinked innocently. *I need to schmoozle the wifey. I'm in so much trouble.*

Silence.

"Babe?" he repeated, then tried his pet name for her. "Jilli-bean?"

"Great, Gid, just great, not that you would know," she responded now. "Do you realise you got home at oh-eight-hundred from The Snake? How you functioned today I have zero idea!"

"Oh, babe," Gid wheedled, "please don't be like that, I functioned well."
He continued proudly: "I made triple-fuelled coffee, then I made our bed,
then I worked an interesting shift today, and then I organised dinner for
us."

But he could tell he was being a little too puffy-chested for her liking. *And
little does she know that I revisited The Snake on my way home after work
for a quick foosball game with the boys.* He conveniently left out that fact
from his list of the day's achievements, and went for changing the subject
completely instead: "Did you hear the alarm today? I feel that something
may be brewing?"

He was sure she knew what he was doing. "Well, thanks babe for the food
prep, but it's easy enough to push a button on our meal replicator," she
scoffed at him, through her clenched jaw. "And no, I didn't get the alarm
memo. Jeez, Gid, you are so paranoid; you must get that seen to sooner
rather than later, yeah?"

Gid ignored her last question. "I adjusted the taste display today; you will
love my new 'recipe', I guarantee, babe. And wait till I tell you what
happened down in the Pit, you won't believe it!"

Lea didn't engage further. Instead she crossed to the drinks replicator, got
something frosty in a tall glass, and downed it in two gulps. It was clear
that she really needed something after a long day at the geosphere.

He watched her and felt a little bit guilty.

His first shift at the Archimedes Pit was so exciting that he had taken a
contract, and six months later it was still just as exciting for him.

But for her… Her work at the geosphere married AI with geology and
herbology, which sounded great to people who didn't know what her
actual job was. The truth was that she was overqualified for her position
and underappreciated in her work.

"I'm worth so much more than a layman's job," Lea sighed to Gid on a
regular basis. "My geosciences PhD is all going to waste."

Gid watched Lea make a second drink, and then a third.

*****

The Line and The Sphere were two newly inhabited purpose-built alternative-community megastructure cities, both of them technologically and sociologically state-of-the-art. Where AI met nature, and everyone who was anyone was vying to buy a residence in one of the two.

The Line was the first of its kind, down on The Surface, in Saudi Arabia. A linear smart city in the desert, 170 kilometres long, home to nine million residents, all under the proud care of Mayor April Baxter. With no cars, streets, currency, pets, crime, or carbon emissions, The Line functioned as a perfect environment for an elite community. A copy of this model, Line 2, was under construction, and another community, called the Eight Rivers Community, was in design concept. But immediately following on from the enormous success of The Line had been The Sphere, an even more elaborate smart-city project, functionally complete but nevertheless under constant development and refinement, even as its population continued to grow. The Sphere represented nothing less than a revolution in urban living; in fact it would be the *new norm* of urban living, if Mayor Eric Anderson (also co-creator of The Sphere) could have his way.

The Sphere differed from The Line in a crucial manner. Its unique Tropic of Cancer location was above the Atlantic Ocean between what were the Florida Keys and the islands of Bermuda. The Sphere was a hovering community with dynamic coordinates, changing daily. Travel to The Sphere was by invitation only, for residents and special visitors. The daily location coordinates would be transmitted as needed, and the journey could be undertaken by teleportation or a special flight craft. The Sphere's 'flight deck' was a complex hologram vortex portal. The Sphere had no physical landing surface area; the purpose-built portals just opened when triggered, so that The Sphere simply seemed to 'absorb' all flight transport that approached it. This technology had been a special project of Eric and his best team, and Eric had taken great pride in it becoming a reality.

At the top of The Sphere was The Apex, from where all government and technological management of The Sphere was coordinated, and it also contained Eric's personal residence. The entirety of the smart running of The Sphere from The Apex was underpinned by an army of purposefully engineered microbots and nanobots that kept both the technological and organic components and residents of The Sphere functional and self-refining. The Sphere was practically a living thing itself, in a perfect symbiosis with its residents. The residents were so 'plugged in' that each human inhabitant had a personal hologram signature and bio-feedback mechanism attuned and attached to their unique biometrics, residences, and communication devices. Together, the people and The Sphere had a single pulse, and represented a shared personality where technology and biology meshed in a never-ending cycle of reciprocal and self-improving feedback.

*****

Lea tasted Gid's dinner effort, and her face lit up.

"Jeez, Gid, you're right!" she gushed. "This is A-MAZING! The chicken is so tender and the flavour is divine!" She savoured the meal between sips of her cocktail.

"Thanks, babe," Gid said happily, enjoying watching her eat. "I was thinking about it and it even distracted me at work. I was mindlessly watching the flying viewer goggles for my last external sweep for the day, and I thought if I instructed the generator to add cinnamon, parsley, any new Sphere-botanicals from the moss gardens – thanks to your brilliance in the herbology projects – and just a splash of vinegar, that would make all the difference, right?"

Lea nodded as she ate, but he didn't mind if she wasn't fully listening. He really was proud of her herbology work, creating genetically specific Sphere-botanicals ('A New Generation of Herbology' was the title of the article that was full of praise for her team). And who cared if some of those on The Surface moaned about 'alien species' being created 'above the Earth'? Most of the new plants were absolutely delicious. Gid enjoyed helping out in the moss gardens and he didn't mind taking a little taste while he did so!

"Well then," he continued, "of course, right at my culinary thought crux, my goggles alarmed, and my temporal transponder triggered too." Each resident's temporal implant had a signature alarm, and the melodic, high-pitched beeps of Gid's alarm still made him jump every time.

Lea laughed as she took her last bites. "Well, thank goodness you don't concentrate at work then! This is delish!" Finally she chuckled and added, "So, spit it out, what happened down in the Pit today with that warning alarm? My temporal didn't go off, so must have been something security-specific, then?"

"Correct…so perhaps I shouldn't tell you," he teased, but continued: "Well, unauthorised drones were inbound, and we found something else, then they were shot down by an I-don't-know-what, just as I zoomed in. And then Eric personally came down from The Apex, so it must have been important."

"WHAT?" Lea exclaimed. "Everyone knows that Eric doesn't involve himself much these days in general concerns."

"Yeah, and," Gid lowered his voice out of habit, "I relayed the thermal heat signature here, then deleted my signature, and the IR images I relayed too, so let's take a look!"

A tingle of excitement hit them both.

"Jeez, Gid," Lea whispered too, "you could get us in a serious security breach doing that, depending on what it is! Did you take it offline?"

"Yes, already did!"

The footage played without audio. They watched images of tiny black spots inbound, then small fireballs descending as if mini explosions were occurring and creating fallout. Multiple drones appeared in the dark, before they disappeared and the sparks cascaded down the apparent glassy surface of The Sphere and fell to the ocean waves below.

"Fuck!" they said together, and then they both jumped violently in unison as the accommodation suite's central command communication lit up and chimed.

"Are you coming to watch the drone skyshow tonight, guys?" came the voice of Randers, their new neighbour. Lea and Gid sat frozen, holding their breaths. "Guys? Hello?"

Gid's temporal alarm sounded, and so did Lea's. The signal was specific – geographical security breach, Lower Level 4.

*****

I'm no longer starting my weeks by wondering what fresh hell each week has to offer...

Gideon's troubles from living on The Surface of Earth seemed to have melted away, and continued to fade from his memory the longer he lived on The Sphere.

I'm so grateful.

After they moved into their Lower Level 4 unit, Gideon would sit in the oceanic window for hours on end. The view was spectacular. "The best of high-rise living, on steroids!" he told his friends. "Scenic views, security, and a sense of community. You can enjoy views of the sunrise and sunset. AI Building Management can take care of any maintenance tasks, so you don't have to do anything." His friends were sold on these praises and many more. They in turn applied for The Sphere, were accepted, and moved in.

Eric is a true genius.

On The Surface, Gideon and Lea had lived on the 'Mainland', far from any oceans. Their home had been quite unique – a London double-decker bus that they parked in an alternative lifestyle community and then turned into a gorgeous off-the-grid tiny home.

But then the home burned down to zilch after a gas bottle explosion, and Gideon had a breakdown.

Lea put him back together piece by piece, then they looked for and found a fresh start. They moved to The Sphere and in their unit they replicated the much-loved double-decker bus accommodation (right down to the layout and the beautiful green paint scheme), and Gideon named their home 'Skyjack'. Even though there were also some Sphere-standard non-bus elements, they were only enhancements, such as the private external balcony-type structure, called a pontoon, that was part of each unit. This was accessed by a voice-activated hatch and consisted of a paired floating platform and overhead canopy shelter, attached to its unit by the same force generator that formed the overall invisible biodome shield of The Sphere, that preserved the city's breathable and comfortable environment even out on the pontoons themselves, and even when The Sphere was higher than the cruising altitude of a commercial plane.

Gideon called his remaining Mainland buddies sometimes, but less and less as time went on – the friends who hadn't followed him to The Sphere couldn't relate to his life now, and he couldn't relate to them. They didn't understand the joy of seeing waves and beaches and whales and ships from the elevation of The Sphere, or the thrill of witnessing a spectacular hurricane passing harmlessly underneath The Sphere that had been raised to escape above it. Sometimes it felt like it was almost as good as going to space, especially after Gid had found that his previous fear of heights had completely disappeared.

Randers was one of Gid and Lea's friends from the Mainland days who had followed them to The Sphere. Randers had made his unit into a Viking longhouse, to honour his ancestry and his childhood home. Randers had said his anxiety was cured too.

*****

"Welcome home, Giddy," said the AI voice of the unit's house manager bot. "I hope you had a good day. The new brass handles are ready."

Giddy seemed to remember that when he had lived on The Surface he was always doing home maintenance. Now, the limit of his involvement was to instruct the house manager, and he could trust that everything would be taken care of. He sure preferred the way things were now.

In fact, the most complicated thing about his life these days was deciding what to tell the house manager to make for dinner, and what flavoured natural syrup he'd like in his sparkling water after work. He didn't miss cooking at all – and talk about your FAST food!

Breakfast the next morning was Turkish eggs, in the most rich garlic and yoghurt sauce, with a side of fresh bourbon bread. Truly the best breakfast in the sky!

Jilly had curled herself up in the window seat, watching the waves below, with her own breakfast of a Nigella's emergency brownie and a cup of cocoa. Her diet was less sophisticated than his, and occasionally even a little bit scandalous, at least by Sphere standards.

He smiled to himself and remembered that one day he had come home earlier than he had said he would and found her sitting cross-legged on the treadmill, eating a packet of old-school chips and drinking a glass of wine. She tried not to look guilty.

"What are you doing?" he grinned at her expression. "Is this what you get up to while I'm at The Snake?"

"Our personal doctor-bot said for me to spend 45 minutes a day on the treadmill..."

"But it probably meant that you should be *moving...*" he was actively laughing at her now. "And where did you get the chips from?"

"Mandy brought them from Sydney when she came to visit, and I stashed them," Jilly was laughing now too. "Oh yes, I'm being a bit naughty tonight, but otherwise I love this life. It's a dream life, don't you think, Giddy?"

His smile had faded a little. "None of the pressures we had in Sydney, I admit that. Everything done for us and available to us and bubble baths every day if we want them, yes. And I do love working in the moss gardens. But I'm still not *sure* about it. Sometimes, I think there has to be MORE..."

Suddenly Jilly stretched in the window seat and spoke, bringing Giddy back from his memories and then accurately guessing where his thoughts had been. "Oh yes, I know that look," she said. "You're questioning our Sphere existence again, aren't you?"

He didn't try to deny it. "It's just that I'm not *sure,* and shouldn't I be sure? It's the same-same. Maybe someday someone will make mischief. No one likes 'smooth' all of the time..."

"Well, I do," Jilly replied.

*****

Darius was a retired theatre actor. His mother had died in his home on The Surface and he couldn't deal with it, so he had sold up and purchased a Sphere residence. Darius hailed from Battery Point in Tasmania. He had spent a fortune on a dilapidated old cottage to renovate, and then could achieve none of it after being caught in a mire of heritage constraints and experiencing insurmountable stress trying to keep the place to its original history. His mother's death had been the final straw, such that the pitch for The Sphere was the perfect ride out of the perfect storm.

LEAVE ALL THE WORK BEHIND, LIVE A LIFE YOU DESERVE, AND BECOME A PART OF ENORMOUS CHANGE!

He had been in his unit on Lower Level 4 for only a couple of weeks, but already he was behaving like a new man, and had even made a friend. He smiled at that friend now, his 'two doors down' neighbour, as they both arrived outside their respective unit doors at the same time.

"Perfect place to live, Gid!" Darius called out. "Most of the time not a soul in sight, just the way I like it!"

"There are more people around if you know where to find them!" laughed Gid in response. "But don't worry, only the kind that you will like. I'll introduce you to the boys at Snake Tavern soon." Darius saluted and entered his unit.

Gid laughed again and entered his own unit, thinking that with both Darius and Randers, Lower Level 4 was turning out to have quite the Bohemian vibe. Gid was glad Darius was settling in so well, and that he was also coming along nicely in his new job in the moss gardens, for which Gid was his supervisor. And when they weren't working and Gid wasn't out at The Snake, they were in training long hours together for the Riot Games, being hosted later in the year at The Line.

Gid wondered if Darius might one day also like to join his periodic bachelor trips to The Surface with Randers, where they visited Ireland

and Scotland, and Gid always made sure to bring back a bottle of excellent Irish whiskey from Donegal.

*****

Lea jumped up, with the alarm still chiming in her temple, and ran to their pontoon hatch. She waved her wrist at the control panel, and to her apparent surprise, the hatch door opened.

"NO! Jilli-bean!" Gideon called to her. "NO!"

He was too late, and could only watch as she went out onto the pontoon platform, and the hatch door closed behind her. Her alarm stopped. Gid was frozen in place, still inside their unit.

Lea saw that their neighbours Darius, Randers and Alfonzo were all standing on their own respective pontoon platforms now, too. They could all see the land of the islands of Bermuda below them.

The form of a plane appeared, flying at an altitude of the underside airspace of The Sphere. The plane was a large passenger airliner, an Airbus A380.

As the Sphere-dwellers watched from their pontoons, a wave of drones appeared and approached the airliner. Darius and Randers both inhaled and choked in horror and Randers exclaimed, "Oh no!"

Suddenly a huge golden orb materialised out of nowhere, low in the sky and spinning and expanding. The airliner flew straight into the orb, which engulfed it completely, and then orb and plane both disappeared.

"What just HAPPENED?" Randers cried.

Alfonzo, one of the very first residents of The Sphere, watched as the drones started to release their fireworks, and casually said, "Welcome to the Bermuda Triangle, folks!"

Lea started to laugh, then suddenly began to scream and clutch and scratch at her face. Randers, two pontoons over, was doing the same. Alfonzo and Darius were shouting too, but they had also quickly pressed their temples and activated instant deployment of protective helmets and body armour, and their shouts were frenzied calls to Randers and Lea to do the same thing.

Gid came to life inside #19 but felt like he was moving with all the pace of a tortoise as he ran to the pontoon hatch door, where he too shouted to Lea. He could see the tiny specks that had attached themselves to her face and hands and were boring into her exposed skin. In slapping at her face she finally activated her helmet and armour. Gid pounded on the pontoon hatch and frantically waved his wrist across the control panel, but the safety protocols would not allow the door to be opened.

Gid watched in horror as Lea looked back at him through the clear face-plate of her helmet, as half of her face flesh sloughed away and her eyes became sightless and dissolved in their sockets. She finally collapsed onto the pontoon platform out of Gid's view.

Gid let out a soft little, "Noooo…" as his own knees buckled and he slid down the inside of the hatch into a crumpled heap on the floor.

Outside, the drones with their fireworks of lasers and nanoweapons finished their cleanup, but the sound of the temporal alarm continued to echo cruelly in Gid's mind for a long time afterwards.

*****

Eric Anderson looked around and then called Gid over to a quiet area of the Pit. Eric held a package out to Gid. "Here, take this to the S1 pontoon. There is a small delivery portal there. I'll give April Baxter at The Line a heads-up that it's coming over for her to receive."

Gid took the package. It felt like it was moving, as if an animal was inside; tiny thud noises, and an unidentifiable humming-type sound.

*****

The sundown drone show was over, and all The Sphere residents who had watched from the public viewing arena made their way back to their habitation levels.

As Gideon and Jili-Bean opened the door of Unit #19, Noodle-Bub, their holo-laser pet-bot companion, jumped up at them. The millions of tiny laser dots danced in perfect alignment to create the illusion of the shape and movements of a cute little dog.

"Lights on!" instructed Gideon, as Jili-Bean knelt and ran her fingers through the lasers representing Noodle-Bub's ears.

Noodle-Bub's mouth representation opened and the sound of a bark was heard. Gideon didn't even wonder anymore how that was possible – he just smiled indulgently as Jili-Bean responded to the bark, cooing softly back to the 'dog', "Aww, Noodle-Bub, I love you, too. You're such great company for me for when Gid goes to The Snake."

*****

Jillibean and Gid watched the illegally obtained images. The footage played without audio, so the only sound in the room was Jillibean slowly chewing her pasta as she stared at the IR screen.

"What IS that?" they finally whispered to each other. On the screen, a large cloud was approaching, but it appeared to be moving with purpose, almost intelligently.

"But The Sphere didn't change its coordinates," Jillibean said, "so it's not a storm cloud, and it doesn't look like one, either. And it's not a large flight vehicle, so what is it?"

"Keep watching," Gid whispered.

A few specks landed on the viewing screen, and then they could see little mechanical eyes, appearing to be looking straight at them.

"OMIGOSH, GID!" Jillibean spat out the last of her ravioli. "It's a cloud of smart particles!"

*****

Gid sat in his seat at Snake Tavern. Quiet. Holding his drink.

"What, are they not serving you whiskey today?" the ribbings flowed in from all the other regulars.

Gid ignored them and sipped his coffee. It was nearly empty.

"No no," said The Snake's owner, who visited his tavern sporadically and sometimes even tended bar. "There is no room in this bar for a coffee machine! We have 280 bottles of liquor on the shelf and over 50 beers on tap. But no, Gid, you want COFFEE?" The owner gave a huge guffaw; his best belly laugh. "You'd better get with the program, mate!"

"No, I have to be able to think straight," Gid muttered.

"That will be a first, Gid!" The roar from the bar regulars followed Gid around the room, while a replay of 'A Nightmare on Elm Street' tried to distract him via the big screens.

Barman Gilbert, observant and subtle, materialised a second cup of coffee for Gid. Gid grabbed Gilbert's sleeve. "What do you know about smart particles?" Gid asked, in an urgent whisper. "And what do you think is missing in our society here?"

An alarm sounded. Security breach.

"Okay, everybody out!" shouted Gilbert.

*****

"Who's operating the quadcopter?" Gid asked the group on the pontoons as they waited for the drone skyshow to begin.

"Not sure," one of them replied, "but did you hear the alarm at The Snake earlier today?"

"Hey, here's a philosophical question," said one of them, presumably to pass the time. Gid saw that it was the newest resident, Alphonse. "What do you think is missing in our society here?"

"Empathy, kindness, compassion and humanity?" replied Gid, still cynical and bitter after the divorce. "Not to mention no more drive-through when we are hungry, no more zipping over to Target to grab toothpaste or Ibuprofen, no more quick fixes needed, no more Alexa writing a book for you... I miss all that."

"Well I sure don't!" exclaimed Alphonse. "I love that all of that's gone, Giddy!"

*****

From high in The Apex, Eric watched a square oscillating wave forming and re-forming in the ocean below. He opened the holographic plan via voice command, hit the button on his communications earpiece, and slapped his hands on the table in satisfied excitement as a call came through.

"You can open the IR file now, the report is ready," he said. He paused for the reply, then with his next breath, added, "Only that situation at The Line is left to finalise. Oh, THAT April Baxter, she is posing as trouble!" He scoffed. "But we can go ahead and take residents at both The Arc and The Orb, and continue with the Terra Experiment."

An alarm sounded, indicating that the package he had given to Gideon to send to April Baxter had just been opened. He gestured to cut the communications call short, as a familiar vibration in his temple signalled a private sub-line call coming through from The Higher Source. The familiar voice came from within his head and congratulated him. He replied inside his mind (but couldn't help smiling and nodding too), "All on track. And make sure to keep all life forms in the dark – we don't need this getting out."

Another standard call was inbound. "Security breach on Lower Level 4, two residents down."

Eric formed his hand into a V-sign, a gesture of affirmation that The Higher Source recognised – palm facing away; a sign of victory.

"The others will appreciate all of this, eventually," Eric spoke softly to himself as he looked out of the window at the repetitive marine squares dancing and intertwining below. He congratulated himself on the perfect frequency.

Another incoming call.

"Hey Eric, there's a brew poured here with your name on it – time to decompress!" a voice chimed. Eric could also make out cheering in the background. "All the boys want you here, too!"

"Zooming in now," Eric replied, swiping the air in front of him and closing his files down.

He activated the Snake Tavern simulation.

He was greeted with many high-fives as he made his way to the bar and chugged his waiting beer. "My shout next!" he called, to a fresh round of cheers.

He took out his custom darts set and grinned around at the regulars. "I've lost track of the schedule – whose turn is it to lose to me tonight?"

*****

They sat at their exterior window, looking out at the approaching aircraft, and watched a square wave that undulated below in the ocean. Micro air vehicles and tiny robotic flying machines bombarded the glass.

Lea's voice was panicked. "What have you done, Gid, what have you DONE? You were being monitored? We're being ATTACKED!"

And then there were explosions.

*****

Eric had successfully sold the concept of The Sphere to the general public, and the desire to take up residency was high. The separate sales pitch to the investors and technology companies had been no less compelling, but a good deal more secretive.

"So the exposure to different and cyclic simulations is what makes our community varied, and in turn the data feedback and learning loop is accelerated, far beyond anything we could achieve naturally," he had summarised. "No one knows what's real and what isn't."

*****

Gideon watched the condensation droplets run down his pint glass as he sat over his beer. The water vapour moved faster than the drink. He circled the glass on the bartop.

"What's the problem today, Gideon?" the new barmaid asked.

"Hmph," Gideon let out, without concern. "I just feel there is trouble coming." His eyes flashed up to the barmaid's smile, and then he continued staring, as he suddenly noticed how pretty she was. "Sorry," he said, "what did you say your name was?"

"I didn't," she replied, still smiling, and then reached over the bartop to shake his hand. "Nice to meet you properly, Gideon. I'm Gillian – Gillian Beenleigh. I'm very new here, just come up from The Surface. I hope you won't hold that against me!"

"Not a chance!" he grinned back. "It's lovely to meet you too, and, well, we were all on The Surface once."

They kept shaking hands as they continued smiling at each other. Gideon liked the soft feel of her hand in his, very much. He was already thinking about when he would ask her out.

3. Mascara.

Emotionally, I was done. Mentally, I was drained. Spiritually, I was dead. Physically, I continued to smile. Disconnected thoughts seemed to circle and dive like seagulls, failing to produce any answers or even to clearly define my equilibrium in this life. Mother had once told me I was made of spare parts, and my first husband had furthered her assertion by stating that I was made with *old* spare parts.

Thank God, then, that a light had come out of the darkness – my soon-to-be second husband was an angel, and happily it had taken me no time at all to figure that out.

*****

Anthony's soon-to-be wife's favourite 'colour' was sunrise – the soft pink hues, the bold golds, and the majestic oranges and reds. She deserved the world, and he was so excited to be marrying her. This would be wife number five for him. He wasn't exactly sure why he couldn't keep them around; he guessed that eventually maybe he felt that he was always desiring more, more, MORE than what they had to offer him. But he would have given each one the world, the universe.

He watched his new fiancée, as she watched the sunrise. She turned and caught him looking. She beamed at him, brighter than the dawn. Then she smirked, and batted her eyes, and said coyly, "You are just marrying me for my amazing eyelashes; don't think I don't know it!"

He laughed, and she giggled back.

"Oh, Lucie," he sighed, "you are a true beauty, my love!"

*****

He raised a glass, full of bubbles. "Cheers to my first official year of you, my angel! Your energy is shining so bright that you belong in the heavens – up there like a sparkling star!"

I thought that Anthony was so ridiculously cute, and I seriously still couldn't believe my luck in finding such a wonderful, beautiful and blessedly attentive husband. "And also a VERY happy birthday to my amazing man!" I responded, as I clinked my own glass against his. "You have brought so much joy and happiness into my life!"

It had turned out that we had the same birthday, so we had thought it fitting to be married on that special day, too.

"Seeing you smile lights me up, and feeling your warmth gives me rest," I gushed, staring into his big brown eyes.

"And now, my gift to you!" Anthony told me, handing me a small shiny box. "Eternal beauty, my angel."

*****

Anthony watched as Lucie opened the gold box and found inside a delicate glass tube with 'My Angel' engraved on it. She turned it gently in her fingers to examine it.

"Oh," she said in surprise, "it's mascara?"

"It's *very fancy* mascara," Anthony said, with a broad smile, and gazed into her eyes in turn. "Only the absolute best for you. And well, you did say I married you for your luscious eyelashes!"

*****

We had met over drinks and nibbles. I was newly divorced, and Anthony was both newly widowed and new to the area. I was still in my post-divorce low, but a colleague had suggested a meet-up. "Well, it can't hurt, just meeting for drinks?" And I had supposed not.

Anthony was handsome, confident, and well-spoken. He had an intriguing accent I couldn't quite place – I found out later it was because he had lived all over the world, and as a result he had picked up the most charming parts of a multitude of accents.

It was an instant attraction.

That was followed by a whirlwind romance, and the next two months had flown by. When I told him my birthday was coming up in August, he had exclaimed that it was his birthday too, on the same day! Then he held both my hands in his and confessed to me that when he had first moved into my neighbourhood, something had compelled him to buy an engagement ring, even before he had unpacked all his moving boxes, and weeks before he even met me. He said that in his mind he was 'manifesting his dreams' (preparation was key!), and then…his dreams had come true. When he told me this, and eagerly asked if we could be married on our shared birthday and go together into the first spring of the rest of our lives, I found that there was no way I could not have said yes.

Anthony insisted that I deserved a gorgeous wedding with sparkling wine and delicious cake and matching bridesmaids and colourful flowers, and all of my friends and family to celebrate us. And that was exactly what happened! Even though it was fast, Anthony planned everything to a tee and my ideal wedding went off without a hitch. It was bliss, and everything that I had ever wanted. We had even taken ballroom dancing lessons after our engagement so that our first dance as a married couple would be perfect. So I walked, and danced, on air.

During our honeymoon he took me to his childhood home to get to know his parents better. They were a little quiet, but welcoming and divine, and seemed to covet me like the daughter they'd always wanted but never had. The visit was wonderful except for some occasional odd moments where Anthony's mother seemed to be annoyed with him for some reason. He apologised to me with, "She is just a little bit cranky at times." She was especially angry one day on the phone and he just hung up on her, and he smiled at me. But nothing was made of it or explained to me further by either Anthony or his mother, and everything otherwise seemed well. In the end the visit was successfully completed with warmth all around, and his mother's farewell hug to me that was flatteringly, sweetly fierce.

We spent the remainder of our honeymoon on a lake, where Anthony had a favourite cabin he had been hiring regularly for all his holidays for many years. And now this latest stay was particularly special, of course. He jokingly introduced me to the lake ducks, his 'friends' that he had known 'since they were eggs'. They seemed glad to make my acquaintance too! More, pure, bliss.

Anthony and I took to married life together like the lake ducks took to water. He was extremely organised around our home. He would cook and clean and shop, and do the garden so that it was perfect for me. He was unfailingly kind and sweet to me; there were never even any of the inconsequential disagreements that any couple living together might normally expect. He pampered me, and I was devoted to him. And we were inseparable. I felt like I really had found an angel, and I was in heaven.

But if I was thinking that Mr and Mrs Anthony Baker must surely, eventually, turn into more of a 'standard' married couple, that never happened.

We threw a joint birthday bash and first wedding anniversary celebration on 11 August. We exchanged presents, ate cake, and watched sports. Later we got dressed up like movie stars and went to a *very* expensive restaurant for dinner, where we also drank a LOT of champagne.

When we got home, Anthony ran me a bubble bath as usual, but the subsequent emergency call for the ambulance was definitely not usual. I had fallen asleep in the bathtub and inhaled some of the water. Perhaps the bath hadn't been the best idea when I was feeling somewhat nauseated that night anyway – too much indulging in rich birthday cake and alcohol, no doubt.

Anthony insisted on sleeping in Lucie's room in the hospital, while she recovered from her misadventure in the bath. He couldn't bear to think that she wouldn't get 24-hour attention without him (the nurses did have other patients to see to, after all). He was discreet, and so solicitous, and the nurses were happy to have him there.

Lucie was discharged after two days, with instructions to take it easy and let her lungs finish their healing. Anthony assured the doctors that he would give Lucie the best of home care. The ward staff all said goodbye to Lucie and Anthony and wished them the best, and those nurses who were single and looking added Anthony's devotion to his wife as an example of what they would like in a partner one day.

*****

A week after I left the hospital my longtime friend Jenna came to visit me, while Anthony was out picking up my prescriptions.

The first thing out of Jenna's mouth was, "I finally timed it well."

"What do you mean?" I queried, through one of my coughing fits.

"Lucie," replied Jenna, "Anthony never leaves you alone, EVER. Every time I see you, he's always with you. Every time I can visit, he's always here." She seemed a little mad. I hadn't taken that much notice, and besides, what did it matter anyway? Anthony was looking after me, and I loved to have him with me.

"I wanted to talk to you alone," Jenna continued.

I almost laughed, but that would make me cough again. "Why? You can say anything in front of him."

"No…" Jenna said, eyeing the doorway somewhat nervously, "actually I feel I can't; he comes off as a little weird to me."

Now I was curious as to what was the matter with her.

"I've done some digging." Jenna winced as if she knew the information she was about to present would not be taken well. "Do you know how many wives he has had?"

"Of course!" I replied. "Anthony and I know all about each other's pasts;

that's no issue for us. He was widowed. Beautiful women. I've seen pictures."

"Well," went on Jenna, "he's been married five times, now. His first wife fell ill and died. Then his second wife was a 24-year-old bride of less than four weeks when she passed away. In her case, apparently two crucial observations were overlooked – signs of a drowning. The third wife fell down the stairs after a long period of mysterious illnesses, and she had cancer symptoms but no diagnosis. And there was froth on her mouth, and water everywhere in their bedroom. Lucie, that's so crazy, and well…I'm so worried for you!"

I was growing more and more incredulous as I listened to this nonsense coming out of my friend, and it was dawning on me just what ugliness she was insinuating. I blurted out, "What the hell?" before my further speech was cut off by another coughing episode.

Jenna continued talking quickly, realising that once I could speak I might not let her finish her piece. "Then, the wife immediately before you, a 28-year-old – and don't you think that's a bit young for a 55-year-old man? – also a drowning. Doesn't that strike you as weird? But I read the paramedic's report from that incident…"

I could find my voice now: "How DARE you say these OUTRAGEOUS things! And how DARE you dig around in Anthony's business…"

Jenna cut me off. "No, listen to me, please listen! If his fourth wife drowned in a bathtub, wouldn't you expect to find evidence of that? But nothing was wet at all! A dry body, dry carpet, dry towels. And all her lotions and bottles by the side of the bath, with not so much as a drop of water on them. I saw the photos, Lucie – it was all so wrong…"

Then I discovered that I could yell, not letting my coughing stop me. "My darling Anthony! He's been through SO MUCH already, so much tragedy, and we've been so happy, and he's looking after me and when I get well we're going to go see the world together… But you, you think you can COME HERE with these accusations! What gives you the right to interfere like this, and why are you making up such lies? Do you hate me? Why do you hate Anthony? Seriously, what's WRONG with you?

Are you JEALOUS?"

Jenna had gone very still. "I care about you," she whispered, tears coming to her eyes. "I'm telling you the truth; the research is real. I've been so worried…so I…I hired a private detective…"

That was the last straw. "You did WHAT? How dare you! No, you're lying! GET OUT! GET OUT!" I screamed. If I could have risen to shove her out of my house, I would have. "Take your crazy delusions out of here; I never want to see you again! Leave me alone! Leave US alone! GET OUT OF OUR LIVES!"

I finally broke down, sobbing and gasping. And my former best friend did as I asked, and exited my home and my life.

*****

After the nasty episode with Jenna, Anthony felt more protective of Lucie than ever. She was not recovering from her bathtub incident as expected, and he was concerned about anything that might upset her. He took a long-term rental on the lake cabin, and moved them there, away from any other so-called 'friends' who might hurt her, away even from any members of their families, while he continued to look after her.

Finally, Lucie was diagnosed with liver cancer.

They commenced her treatment at the local hospital, and Anthony took an extended leave of absence from his job so that he could devote himself full-time to Lucie.

"I love you so much, and you're so good to me," Lucie said to him, every day, as he measured her medicine and changed her sheets and cooked special food and rubbed soothing cream into her skin and painted her nails and held her to him.

"My darling, my angel," he replied, and kissed her very gently, "I love you too, and it's my privilege to look after you."

*****

The closer I would get to treatment days, I'd cry more often. I fell more, and preferred to stay seated as much as possible, as I consistently could not catch my breath.

Anthony was wonderful, and I told him so all the time. He would take my elbow to help me walk; he brought me heat packs when I needed them, then ice packs at other times. He did everything for me, and he was everything to me.

I felt like my 'spare parts body' was really failing me; maybe Mother was right all along. I once was healthy and strong, but now…not. My husband was my shining star, and he was always there for me. My friends had either rudely removed themselves from my life or just faded away, but the connection I felt with my husband was my one true gift.

"Thank you for being here with me," I told Anthony daily, as he kissed my lips so lightly, and gently rubbed my back.

"I wouldn't want to be anywhere else," he would reply softly.

I loved him so much; he spent so much time caring for me and idolising me. On the especially bad days, he would bring me homemade soups, and spoon-feed me, and look at me so tenderly. I never wanted this love to end, and with his care, I hoped I could get many more years to just stare into his dreamy loving eyes.

Anthony approached me as I was resting in my favourite chair, in the morning sun. He carried a handful of jars and tubes – I knew what that meant. I smiled at him, and he smiled back at me.

"It's a beautiful day," he said, bending down to kiss me, "and you are beautiful. Here, let me pamper you. I'll pop on your favourite face-cream, and your anniversary mascara too – enhance those amazing lashes. That will make you feel good!"

"Oh, yes," I sighed, patting his hand lovingly. "I particularly like those, they smell like almonds."

Anthony continued to pamper me, and love me, and always tell me I was beautiful, even as I grew sicker day by day. My eyes would sting all the time, now – I cried whenever Anthony wasn't looking at me.

I came to realise, at the end of my life, that what really mattered was not what we bought but what we built; not what we got but what we shared; not our competence of character; and not our successes, but our significance. Live a life that matters. Live a life of love, even if it's for a shorter time than you had expected, for time really expands when love fills you, and wanting more of that is bliss. MORE.

I embodied all this bliss, and my love with Anthony embodied all this bliss. I felt it shining bright, and I took comfort in knowing that Anthony would take it with him afterwards, for both of us.

*****

Through yet another flood of tears, after standing outside on the cabin patio gazing up and wishing upon all those gorgeous stars twinkling in the sky, Anthony gathered up Lucie's belongings.

He set the cache of hyaluronic serum bottles, face-cream jars, and mascara tubes aside. He put on his gloves and mask, then carefully added the cyanide, sulphur, selenium and more into the relevant tubes and jars and bottles, and mixed their contents well. Finally he placed the new manufacturer's stickers on to give the appearance of unused products, and placed the cosmetics in the manufacturer's decorative gold boxes.

Now…to find wife number six…

He needed MORE to love, craved more to care for, more to covet, more to whom to offer his world and give to the universe, MORE to give his own life its very unique purpose and meaning.

At last everything that needed to be packed up was ready. He finished loading the car and got in, and began to drive.

The Beatles song 'Lucy in the Sky With Diamonds' played on the radio. *Oh, how appropriate.*

He felt his mood and his hopes lifting, and sang along with the radio as he double-checked that his new passport, back in the name of 'Finn MacKinnon', was tucked safely in his carry-on bag on the passenger seat beside him. Soon, Finn would be boarding a flight to the UK. He looked forward to finding more sunrises at home in the Scottish Highlands where he had been born.

4. Grilling.

I forget, sometimes, that one day I too will only be a memory.

As long as there is love, there will be grief.

This was actually the title of a poem, by psychologist and author Heidi Priebe, that I had found randomly while browsing the internet. I had shared it with Suzi, and she had really loved it. I had then seen the sentiment sprinkled around on her social media posts, several times after that.

And now I was seeing it again, on a Post-it note, in the familiar bubbly handwriting. I just stared, and couldn't put it down. Suzi had liked to write little lines to herself on Post-it notes. Whenever I found another one, years after she was gone, it was so special but still so raw for me. Just when I felt I had pulled myself together, another memory would burst over me like a flood. I sighed.

I know you get tested the most when it's time for you to evaluate and evolve, but do NOT break. I told myself this, over and over.

I've cried enough tears to fill an ocean (someone get Hallmark on the line!). And freelance journalism was hard even at the best of times. When I was writing about Suzi, it was as a professional, but it was also as her dearest friend…so sometimes, I found myself lost for words.

I was already in the kitchen, with my laptop at the table. Easy enough to make myself a stimulating cup of tea to help me work.

> *Sam and Suzi had so much life ahead of them before they died in a motor vehicle accident in early May, just weeks after Sam proposed to Suzi. But in the months following, their loved ones learned more about them with the ways they had already left their marks on both the world and within their small community of York's Landing. Years on is no different.*

No – terrible writing. I deleted it, and tried again.

> *They had it all figured out, and were blissfully living out their dreams. Unlike yours truly, who still had to look twice to make sure she hadn't put her socks on inside out.*

Hmmm, maybe… But this was HARD.

I sipped my tea, thinking about Suzi, remembering her, wondering what words could possibly honor her, and waited for inspiration to arrive.

*****

Every day, Suzi would spend much of her time harvesting a species of cactus that was edible. Sam, when he was home from the Navy, would do push-ups, under the supervision of their elderly German shepherd rescue dog, Buddy (who was called that because Sam had a quirky sense of humor when it came to dog names – Sam or Suzi always ended up having to explain to people that this Buddy was a girl). Super Mario was also a constant feature of their lives, as Suzi and Sam relived their lost childhoods. Sam's father was a keen Mario fan, and when Sam was a boy he and his father had played the game nearly daily. So now Suzi was happy to assist Sam with whatever joy could be created with a gaming console.

Suzi was always making plans and dreaming of their life together.

"We are already living our dream life together!" Sam would respond whenever Suzi started describing her goals and desires for their future. "This is IT, woman!"

"Yes, it's a beautiful life," Suzi would smile, with great love and passion. "But eventually I would like to get married, and I can't wait to have kids, and can't we also move to a dry and dusty place where we can have an actual cactus farm of our own?"

And then Sam would feel guilty for thinking, *Gee, it's never enough for her – she always wants more, no matter where we are right now.*

"We are grilling tonight!" Suzi shouted out from the back porch as soon as she heard Sam pull up in the old wagon. And then she muttered to herself, "That stupid truck will be the death of us." She wondered why he didn't just take his bike – he loved that bike – but she never said anything to him in case she hurt his feelings. He hadn't been quite the same since his father's death a couple of years ago, right after they had lost their girl Buddy.

"Yes, grilling is soul healing!" Sam called back to her. "We need to have some meat as well as your cactus steaks!" He shunted his new slimline sunglasses away from his eyes, and balanced them off the end of his nose. It was a particularly hot summer for York's Landing.

Suzi always had something new to tell Sam, every day. Sometimes she would be positively bouncy about it.

"I feel empowered when I'm cleansed and strong," she exclaimed to Sam one evening, as their last spring was beginning. "I've been getting Sparky York to come by and work his magic on the greenhouse – I hope that's OK. And I'm crushing the cactus now and making juice and I'll be selling it on Main Street, through Lyndsey's store. I'm so excited!"

Sam laughed at her enthusiasm, and this encouraged her to continue: "See, if we lived in a dry place my cacti would grow more prolifically." She looked at him hopefully. Sam just smiled, and knew that it would never happen. But he could give her something else, instead.

Sam had finally formally proposed, and Suzi was ecstatic. She was also very happy to be able to take Sam's surname at last. She had in fact dropped her own surname years ago, because it was a famous name, though she wasn't famous herself. All the Hollywood kids had seemed to be going mononymous in those days, so she had thought that was good enough for her, too.

Now she would have a new name, and a new family history. Sam was of Italian descent and he had an Italian surname to prove it. But if that wasn't enough, he also made great Italian food, especially pasta. In the winter when it was far too cold out for grilling, or on very special occasions, Sam would take pasta requests from her. When she had decided what she wanted, he would fish around in his memory for his best appropriate pasta recipe.

She would then watch him make the meal, for what felt like hours, as though time was standing still. He even made the pasta itself from scratch, starting with circling his finger in a mound of flour on the bench – no store-bought dried noodles would do. But he created magic, and each bite of the resulting dish was like an Italian adventure.

As the weather continued to warm, bringing the promise of summer, Suzi and her bestie Lyndsey resumed their regular girls-only picnics. Suzi always said food tasted better outdoors, and that went for picnics just as well as grilling. Plus it seemed important to have as much fun together while they were still two single girls, although they both knew that nothing would stop them continuing to hang out together even after Suzi was married.

Suzi had brought along a tiny portion of Sam's latest pasta masterpiece, for Lyndsey to try. And even though the leftovers were cold, Lyndsey's tongue could still taste the bold Tuscan sunrises and sunsets, and the sweetness of the Italian valleys.

"Oh my GOD!" exclaimed Lyndsey, as Suzi grinned knowingly and nodded. "How do you not ask him to make this for you three meals a day? I mean, no offense to your cactus steaks, but…"

Suzi laughed out loud, and replied, "I think he could be a world-famous chef, if he wanted to. And perhaps he does."

"Look, Suzi," said Lyndsey, laughing as well, "I love you to bits, but if anything ever happens to you, I'll be marrying Sam myself!"

Because Suzi loved Lyndsey to bits too, she knew exactly how to take that. She responded, "No, fuck that! If anything ever happens to SAM, I'm marrying YOU instead!"

"Yesss!" Lyndsey pumped her fist.

"And then we'll run away together to Scotland!" shouted Suzi, showing that she knew Lyndsey well.

They both collapsed in a heap of giggles, then lay flat on the grass, running the cool blades through their fingers and discussing the cactus product sales at Lyndsey's store.

Eventually Lyndsey sat back up and grabbed the last of the cold pasta, cramming it into her mouth and smiling back at Suzi. "Oh, I really really HAVE to try this hot and fresh – please please can I come to dinner soon, like really soon?" she mock-begged.

"OF COURSE!" squealed Suzi. "Next week, for sure!"

But that week never came. Or at least, it did, but not with Sam and Suzi in it.

*****

My tea had cooled, and my cheeks were wet. "Suzi…we still talk about you…" I whispered. The kitchen fell silent again, until my nails began tapping on my laptop keyboard. The words flowed out automatically, intuitively. I gulped a mouthful of the cold tea.

The sun was setting, casting a long shadow across the winding coastal road, as Sam gripped the handlebars of his beloved Harley. Suzi cuddled in behind him, holding on tight. Sam took the corners a little too fast but they both loved the adrenaline pumping. It was date night, and a long ride to a seaside restaurant seemed fitting.

The kitchen tap turned on, startling me into stopping typing. I frowned and watched the water stream out of the end of the tap. Then the water stopped, abruptly, by itself. I blinked.
"Hello?" I whispered, looking all around. Nothing. *Of course. Silly.*
I shook my head and resumed typing.
The TV in the lounge room behind me turned on. I saw it come alive, reflected in my computer screen. As the TV reflection started switching between channels, I got up and faced into the lounge room. The TV screen was now pitch black, with white bold writing flashing across it...

I KNOW.

"HELLO?" I squeaked, in a too-high voice.
The TV flashed and flashed its white lettering on the black screen.

I KNOW.
I KNOW.
I KNOW.

And then nothing. The TV turned off. For a few minutes, I was frozen with fear, with anticipation. Finally I felt able to move, and I went outside, shaking and feeling sick. I took a few deep breaths of the fresh night air, and then made my way warily back inside, not knowing what to expect. I looked around carefully; nothing looked strange or out of place. Letting out a huge sigh, I scolded myself for my too-vivid imagination. I sat back down at my laptop.

Death can be convenient.

There it was, on the computer screen. But I hadn't typed it. Had I? Had someone else?

I looked around again, ridiculously scared at that moment. I couldn't see anyone else, or anything unusual, with sinks or with entertainment appliances or with anything else. Maybe my 'intuitive typing' had taken over while I was disturbed about the tap and the TV? I hit 'undo' and my few lines of article that I remembered actually typing reappeared on the screen. Good, but I was done with journalism for right now.

I cocooned myself that night, tightly rolled in my bed covers, feeling completely freaked out by the evening's events, and a little afraid to go to sleep. "Spooks!" my mother would have said. I had – HAD – believed I was of a different school of thought.

My eyes eventually closed.

I saw my late little doggie, Charlie, my spaniel, my best friend during my school years, eating my philosophy textbook. And then I saw a familiar woman, a beloved woman, sitting on the stonework fence of my walled garden, and staring out across the fields and to the mountain peaks beyond. I heard myself shouting: "SUZI! SUZI!"

I awoke with a start, coughing and spluttering, and I still heard myself calling to her: "Suzi! Suzi! SOOOOOOZ!"

I ran out into the lounge room and found that the TV was on, and playing an old video, showing Suzi at one of our girlie picnics. I was filming her running around, and I was calling out, calling, calling to her always… "SOOOOOOZ!"

I giggled, almost hysterically, as the view changed to selfie-mode, and there we both were, on the TV screen, smiling and making kissy mouths at the camera.

"Suzi, I still talk about you," I whispered.

The TV screen instantly changed to black, and then those same white letters, just as before, began flashing.

I KNOW.
I KNOW.
I KNOW.

I froze again.

"Suzi?" I finally whispered, into the infinity. The flashing letters on the TV immediately changed.

I'M HERE, LYNDS.

I screamed and screamed and ran outside, even peeing myself a little. I stood out in the walled garden, trembling. I heard Charlie panting. *What the actual fuck?*

The moon was full, and high in the sky. I thought I could see shadows of someone walking around inside my home. I ran on shaky legs to my neighbor's house, and we called the police, and I stayed with my neighbor for the rest of the night.

The police left my home at sunrise, without having found any intruders or anything unusual. I waited with my neighbor until my mother, roused from her own bed by my frantic pre-dawn call, arrived.

My mother moved in with me for a while, and looked after me, and looked after my store, while I took a break. From everything.

*****

Late one sunny afternoon, after my mother had been with me about two weeks, I went out onto my decking area within the walled garden. I had treated myself to a new patio setting, and now I happily sank down into one of its plump seat cushions, and placed my laptop on the thick glass top of the outdoor table. It was time to get back to journalism.

I opened my laptop, and brought up the draft file of my last article.

There was no time for a goodbye. I was so sad about that; I still am. And about no more picnics, no more ice cream by the bay, no more of our special chats.

Often there is no one here, just the way I like it. Death is convenient, but it was also unexpected. I thought I had more time. But that's what we all say, on this side of the fence.

Even though I had loved and respected Sam, sometimes I also wondered if I could ever really understand him...

As we neared that sharp corner, the familiar thrill of the ride had momentarily faded. Sam was glancing at the speedometer, at the needle hovering at just about the limit. And I had shouted, "Shit, Sam!" The asphalt seemed slick, and I thought what a near miss that was. I could feel Sam's heart pounding, as hard as mine was, from under his jacket.

Then in that instant, Sam was hurtling through the air, the bike sliding out from under both of us, and throwing him ahead of the impending skid and crush on the gravel shoulder. The world seemed to slow down. The sound of the engine sputtering, and a screech of oncoming brakes, filled my ears just before the thud of the impact.

There was no pain. I expected there would be searing pain, but there was nothing, just blackness. And then light. I had stood up and shaken myself off and looked for Sam, spotting him as he stood up by the near embankment.

"YOU OK?" I shouted out.

"YES, YOU?" he answered. He had limped over to me, and then we just stood there, staring, and dumbfounded.

The color of the fading light made way for a beautiful sunset. We were looking down at our bodies. I was trapped under the bike, which lay sandwiched under the front end of the truck. Sam was lying in the gravel of the side shoulder. We watched the truck driver jump out of his rig – first he checked Sam's

body, and then he checked mine, and then he got dazedly back
into his truck and called for help.
Sam and I stared at the bodies, and at each other, somehow also
standing there, witness to our own corporeal conclusion. We
could no longer 'talk' but I had felt Sam's words inside my
head, because they were my words, too: "I thought we had more
time."
Now, Sam has gone.
But I'm still here, Lynds. With you. I get to stay.
I leave signs for you, Lynds, everywhere. Why don't you watch
the TV much these days?
Don't be afraid. There's no need to be afraid.
Go look at the fridge.

I was mesmerized, reading the whole thing, and only when I reached the end was the spell broken, and I slammed my laptop shut. I stared, out over the fields, for several minutes.

I reopened my laptop. The writing was still there. I hit 'undo' but the writing stayed. I hit 'undo' again. Now there was a blank page. But before I could be relieved, new typing appeared, by itself, letter by letter.

TRUST ME

I jumped up and screamed.

STOP IT, LYNDS

"What's wrong, honey?" my mother called, from the kitchen. "You OK out there, Lyndsey?"
I didn't reply, but my mother could see me from the kitchen door now, where she stood with her arms full of things, and she was satisfied that I seemed to be all right.

My mother came out to me on the deck, and I saw that she was carrying barbecue items. "I got your message," she smiled at me. "We are grilling tonight!"

She started unloading tongs, a tray, mushrooms, chicken, and cactus steaks onto the glass-topped table. "That was very cute," she said, "your message on the fridge. Just like something Suzi would do, bless her soul. And a wonderful idea!" She moved to the little barbecue at the end of the decking, began the business of starting it up, and nodded to me. "You finish up your work, and I'll get grilling, in honor of Suzi."

I nodded in reply, still not trusting myself to speak, but my mother didn't seem to notice. I came out of my daze enough to go inside, into the kitchen. I went over to the fridge.

My fridge was no different to many other fridges in the world, I'd guess – covered in fridge magnets of various kinds, including a whole lot of those colorful plastic-coated magnetic alphabet letters that kids (and adult kids…) like to play with. I'd been to the fridge earlier in the day, to get milk for my tea. The message I could see spelled out in the uppercase magnetic letters, prominently near the top of the fridge door, had certainly not been there before.

GRILLING CACTUS STEAKS TONIGHT

"Suzi?" I whispered, yet again. My eyes widened as I watched the lowercase alphabet magnets slowly shuffling themselves on the fridge door, right in front of me.

yes lynds

"I don't… I can't… No way, SUZI?"
More shuffling.

no freak out

"This can't be happening, surely?" I asked, but I was almost coming to understand that it could.

it is

"Have you been leaving me Post-it notes, that I thought were old ones? Did you type on my laptop, and was it you on the TV and playing with the kitchen tap, too?"

yes i live

"You…you 'live'? You mean here? Are you staying?"

i can
if you ok

My head whirled. I was…I was *talking* to Suzi. No, talking *with* Suzi. My lost bestie. *This was real. THIS WAS REAL!* Suddenly I wasn't frightened anymore, just so very GLAD.
"How do we do this?"

pretend

"Pretend you are alive?"

yes

"Yes…"

*****

The subsequent summer, another unusually hot one, was so different when compared to the previous one. I couldn't go on a picnic with Suzi again, but now it didn't seem to matter, and didn't make me ache like it had previously. At home when I caught my reflection in a mirror, sometimes I thought I saw Suzi. And if I asked, "Is that you?" often the TV would turn on and I would see some reassuring flashing white letters on the dark screen. The fridge magnets continued to move, and for any really in-depth 'conversations' we wanted to have, the laptop would come out and the typing on the screen would bring me a joy I never thought I would experience again.

Over the past few days, sometimes I had felt like an invisible waterfall of warmth was cascading over me, gently, almost protectively. Each time it happened, it would tingle and flow through me, like when I was cold and would take a drink of hot tea. It was wonderful. It made me realize that death was not necessarily what we 'knew' it to be, as an ending – it was just a different kind of beginning.

If I could, I would still bring Suzi back to life, no question, in a heartbeat. I still grieved for what we had had then, but I also appreciated what we had been given now, and I found a measure of contentment in that.

I thought more and more these days of the last two lines of the Heidi Priebe poem that Suzi and I both loved. They did hit a little differently to me now.

> *Grief is a giant neon sign, protruding through everything, pointing everywhere, broadcasting loudly, "Love was here."*
> *In the finer print, quietly, "Love still is."*

And I would smile to myself, because my finer print was created with fridge magnets. Love still is, here…

<u>York's Landing Tribune:</u> **GRILLING, by Lyndsey Lake**

They had it all figured out, and were blissfully living out their dreams. Unlike yours truly, who still had to look twice to make sure she hadn't put her socks on inside out.

The sun was setting, casting a long shadow across the winding coastal road, as Sam gripped the handlebars of his beloved Harley. Suzi cuddled in behind him, holding on tight. Sam took the corners a little too fast but they both loved the adrenaline pumping. It was date night, and a long ride to a seaside restaurant seemed fitting.

The world seemed to slow down for them at that moment, as the sound of their engine sputtering and the screech of oncoming brakes filled their ears.

They thought they had more time, but they found the light. Death may be unexpected, but it's not the end, it's another beginning.

I honor my best friend like she is still living here with me. I now run her business of making cactus steaks and cactus juice (I even have a cactus-harvesting team!). We sell her cactus products at my health food store on Main Street, in York's Landing. I'm sure you know the store – it used to have another name, but now, it is simply called: SUZI'S.

Suzi and I hope to see you there – come say Hi to us, and grab a few of her beautiful cactus steaks.

And let's all get **GRILLING.**

5. Yellow Dress.

She could tell it was going to be a perfect beach day. The seagulls sang a particular melodic song in unison, not the usual low piercing *kee-oww*. The breeze smelled like jasmine. Most of all, it just felt right.

*****

A lot of her days often didn't feel right.

Angelique was famous in a way that a beautiful lady can be in a small circle, in a small town. She was a 'career waitress', and no one understood her, except for Neale. The sleepy coastal backwater was not a place to meet Mr Right, but Angelique had no intention of meeting another man. 'The one', years ago, had been perfect, but too much.

Never again, she promised herself.

"Men are trouble!" she would repeat to herself.

Over the years she had discovered that everyone in this town was either a cousin of another, or a second cousin, or some other distant relative. Visitors to the area were the only 'potentials', but they all seemed to be uppity city folk day-tripping – enjoying their oat milk lattes, the organic roadside produce stalls, and the idyllic scenery of Berry Point. Angelique had never left Berry Point, ever, and didn't see why she ever would.

*****

Neale had a lot of friends but no one ever asked him outright why he hadn't formally introduced Angelique, the stunner, to any of them. Neale was ordinary, somewhat strange, and his only passion was to use his metal detector on the beach and hoard the discarded treasures in a little beach shack that no one knew about, a good sixty-minute walk from Far Beach, past the interstate rail line, where the oyster shells lay.

"Are you kidding? You're confident enough to strike up a conversation with her," he scoffed to his mates.

"Yeah, but bro…that day that Angelique looked at me right in my eyes, bro…her eyes are wild, she just scares people off."

"Yeah, you wouldn't get through her walls," Neale echoed, intentionally putting them off.

Her voice trailed off in his head, as it often did. "I'm scared, Neale, really scared. How do I ever heal from the past? I don't know what love is, anymore, do I?"

He loved that her hair was winter fire, and how the bulk of the flames cascaded over her shoulders after being tied back at the nape of her neck for her restaurant shift. He recalled walking her home after sitting there for hours ordering coffee.

"How can you drink so much in one sitting? Your liver is going to be shot!"

It was love at first sight for Neale, but he had no chance with her and he knew it. Once, THAT surfer-fella had come to town and stolen her heart. Depression had hit for Neale. But then, the heart-thief had walked into the water at Far Beach – after drinking himself into a stupor and swallowing three packets of…something – and had vanished after swimming off beyond the point. And Neale was there for Angelique, witnessing her heart come home, but shattered into a million pieces, all bundled up in a yellow dress.

She said for years following that she never felt right.

*****

The sand was squeaky, and warm – not like the heat of summer that burns bare toes, but warm enough for the heat to penetrate the towel to warm her back and feel like a heat pack from head-to-toe. A repetitive 'bleep bleep' sound caught her ears as it hung on the wind from down the beach. No sooner had she sat up than Neale scooted in next to her, missing the towel entirely and spraying her with sand so that her teeth crunched.

"Thanks for being my unpaid therapist, again," she winked.

"Always!" He smiled at her with his crooked smile. "One day, let's flip a coin. Heads, I'm yours. Tails, you're mine!" He offered his best belly laugh.

"Ha, you wish," she said, as she continued to spit out the last grains of sand. "Oh, Neale, you make me laugh. But no more bringing ice-cream cones to me when I'm in the toilet – even if it's melting all down your hand!"

"Well, I didn't want you to miss out, Ange!"

They both giggled, and locked eyes.

"We are great together," said Neale, "and one day, after we get old and dithery, I want you to write on my gravestone, 'I FEEL THE ZOO WHEN I'M WITH YOU'."

"The zoo?"

"Yes. I don't just feel butterflies when I'm around you, Ange, I feel the whole zoo!"

She frowned and dropped her eyes from his. Then she jumped up, grabbing her towel, and quickly disappeared up the pathway.

Well, that one comment spoiled my beach time. MEN!

*****

Angelique would never voice to anyone, or even repeat it to herself, that her biggest wish was to feel, really FEEL, love again. She always looked forward to going home, walking through her door, and being greeted with the warmest of feline purrs – that was love. Her three cats would wind themselves so adoringly around her ankles, tiptoe stealthily around her…and then extend their spines to sprawl over her like a blanket. Sitting there patting them was relaxing and soothing, symbiotic no doubt for all involved, and reduced her stress.

She looked to her right and into the hallway's elongated antique mirror on the wall.

"So interesting what people choose to stress over…" she said to her reflection. "I've prayed and believed my whole life, and yet here I am, mid-thirties, alone and unloved. I am the nicest person I know, and also the meanest, and my life is perfect, but still not enough."

She frowned at herself and gazed deeper into the mirror, into her green eyes, noticing what looked like a flame in her left iris. She blinked, and peered deeper still.

"You've lived a life free of trouble, for the most part. But your existence is like a prison cell and you accept it; nice and comfy, and there doesn't seem to be any need to leave. The door is wide open until time runs out…then it's too late and the opportunities disappear..."

An image of a lady in a yellow dress formed in her mind, the same lady she had seen when she was a small child, standing in the living room of this very family home, right down the end of Tenth Street near the railroad. The same lady who was now talking back to her, reflected in the mirror, with reflected flames also in her eyes.

*****

"I don't remember when I first heard the story, Neale," she said, as she sipped some coffee at a quiet corner table, "but I remember it from the first time I heard it. And by that I mean it made an impression on me, but I had forgotten until I saw her in the mirror last night!" She exhaled in one long breath.

"A vision?"

"A VISION? No, no, it's more than that! Oh, Neale!" She ticked her tongue between her teeth, flicked her flaming ponytail, and rose from the table.

As she hastened away, she muttered under her breath, "Friggin' men, no idea about anything!"

Frustration was building. "Can't trust anyone around here!" she yelled through the servery window at Barry in the restaurant kitchen, while she waited for the next order-up.

Barry didn't respond. He was used to her ranting.

*****

The local senior constable walked into the restaurant and questioned every table after receiving the call that Angelique had never made it to work on Monday. He informed them that he wouldn't be filing a missing persons report until she was missing for 24 hours.

"That's ridiculous! The first 24 hours are crucial, aren't they?" asked Barry, Angelique's employer for the past 15 years. "We need to find her, safe and well. She doesn't have anyone else."

"She was around at the beginning of last week, but we haven't seen her for a while. Even days, maybe," said a table of Neale's friends.

A cohort of worried restaurant colleagues finally convinced the reluctant senior constable to check out Angelique's home, down past the railroad tracks, and they even accompanied him there. They peered in through her front windows.

"Creepy place," said one.

"Yeah, I don't how she can stay here. It's haunted, you know?" said another.

"Well, it was her mother's childhood home," Barry said, "and a long line of the Yellow family has lived here before that. Really nice people."

"Doesn't she have cats?" the senior constable queried. "You'd think they would be hungry and racing around if she was missing?"

"She does, yes, a few I believe."

"Well, she must be around; I can't see any upset cats. Let's see if she turns up tomorrow then, and we will take it from there." And the senior constable left.

Angelique's co-workers looked around at each other.

"I don't like this! I feel something isn't right!" cried out one of the other waitresses.

"I don't like it either." Barry was markedly concerned. "She would never miss a shift. She hasn't just never shown up in fifteen years, and she always lets me know anything that's going on with her and her life issues."

They went around to the back door. Cat fluff was all over the back stairs. There was blood on the bottom step. They could see Angelique's beach bag open on the ground by the back fence, with its contents strewn from the bottom step all the way to the fence, on the train-track side.

"Oh, this doesn't look good, something is definitely wrong!"

So they called the senior constable back, and he was forced to take things seriously at last. Sirens wailed and a search team was organised. A grid was established north of the railroad tracks and a group of volunteers began to walk along the tracks as far as they could see.

"I've found her purse and her ID!" exclaimed one volunteer, almost immediately.

Another soon shouted: "And here are her shoes, with what looks like a dark substance, maybe blood? And ginger cat fluff, too."

*****

"Why do I feel this way?" Angelique asked rhetorically, talking into the mirror next to the sink. Her three cats wound themselves around her ankles as she made her way to the table and sat. Her ginger boy leapt up onto her lap and she stroked his bare patch; she felt so bad that she had been a little rough squashing them all into the carrier so quickly. "It's okay, babies, Mummy is sorry."

Neale entered through the back door of the shack. She hugged him. The cats acknowledged him but didn't offer any affection his way.
"I love that you're hiding out here!" Neale sighed. "You should do it more often."
"I love it here, Neale. It feels like home; more than my house ever feels." She smiled the sweetest smile, and stared into his eyes. "I miss you when you're not here…why do I feel that way?"
"It's called love, Angelique," Neale held her hand so gently in his. "I love you even more than I annoy you. Which is a lot."
She smiled and giggled; her heart was full.
"Love is a friendship set to music," he said. "Or to a metal detector's beeping, too. Right?"
"It does feel right, so right, at the beach shack," she confessed.
He smiled back. He lifted the little frills on her yellow dress, as the trio-of-fur organised themselves on the rattan chair right next to her. Neale picked up the mustard layers of fabric and let them go playfully, as he handed her a freshly plucked sprig of jasmine from the front fence.

Something caught Angelique's eye, and a flickering light made little flames dance in her irises.
She went out to the back of the shack, her feet sinking in the sand. Something was glinting in the long grass behind the outhouse. Seagulls flew in at the sight of her, and perched on the crumbling fence posts. She froze. So confused. Blinking at the direct sun.
She looked behind her and Neale was waving from the small shack window. Ginger jumped up to the windowsill, and Neale patted him with his free hand. Neale stopped waving and gave Angelique a thumbs-up gesture instead, mouthing, *IT'S OKAY.*

A sudden flood of familiarity drenched her; she had done this before. Small pebbles and shells glinted in the sun. Even a well-weathered spoon sat cemented into the top of a gravestone.

I FEEL THE ZOO WHEN I'M WITH YOU
Neale Walker, 1972-2001
Beloved husband of Angelique Yellow-Walker
Forever at sea, forever at our shack

6. The Owls are Always Watching.

There is nothing more enjoyable in life than a good funny story. A good old laugh at something or someone, or at yourself, for that matter! Does that extend to electric fences? Not usually, I tell myself, but after my most recent housesitting job, it's become the usual. I mean, housesitting a farm…what could go wrong?

*****

Amity had left earlier, a couple of hours before I was supposed to start my caretaking. Mika, her husband, had also left earlier than expected, so that when I arrived at the hobby farm it was to be greeted only by the house pets. And they were adorable!

First, Spice-the-Dalmatian bounced out of the laundry room, nearly bowling me over as she skidded sideways on the polished oak floor, leaving a large gouge, before ploughing into the white couch.

Trinity-the-kitten initially came hot on Spice's heels, but abruptly changed direction to fly past me and up the curtains at full speed, where she dangled precariously from the top, looking back down at me.

"Goodness, guys!" I gushed and frowned all at once at the enthusiastic welcoming committee.

I looked around and found a letter from Amity and Mika, sitting on the kitchen bench. An early sentence was underlined and immediately caught my eye.

> *Don't let Spice run too fast inside or she will scratch up our new oak floors, and Trinity will absolutely destroy the curtains if you don't keep her away from them.*

Oh no – 101 fails in the first five minutes!

*****

The century-old farmhouse exterior was not a representation of the home's interior. Its extensive internal renovation was a mixture of gorgeous historic design and modern bits and bobs. It seemed maximised for dust collection, and it gave me a lot of glass to clean. Argh!

But that first evening was idyllic. I sat in the lounge room in front of a roaring open fire, with Trinity and Spice by my feet. Our bellies were full from a hearty home-cooked meal, and all seemed well. I felt myself starting to doze.

> *Trinity likes to wake the household up at three o'clock in the morning with her random-flights-of-fancy hallway-scuttling, so put her to bed in the laundry at night.*

I got Trinity cosily settled in her little 'suite' in the laundry. Then I plastered on a thick layer of my favourite overnight face-cream, and headed upstairs to bed.

Spice is allowed upstairs with you only when you go to bed. If left unattended she will sleep on ALL of the beds.

Spice didn't need to be invited upstairs. She bounded up the steep ascent ahead of me, hugging the long glass balustrade so closely she left a wet slobber streak along its entirety, all the way to the top. Her little nose squelched and crunched as she seemed to ensure to smear the full surface of the glass.

She stopped in her tracks on the top landing, eyeballing me with those wide amber eyes as she froze on the spot, seemingly waiting for my scolding. Then she gave the glass one final lick as if to emphasise my needing to clean it, and disappeared into the master bedroom before I could say anything.

I followed her in. There she was, a gorgeous black-and-white spotted beast, sprawled out on the king bed and snuggled into its black silk sheets. She barked in a satisfied way.

"I'm not sure if you are allowed up there, girl?" I questioned, probably rhetorically.

I gently sat next to her, intending to reach under her so she would jump down. The shiny sheets offered a puff of air as I sat, and a fine cloud of Dalmatian hair plumed upwards, then stuck to my creamy face as it floated back down. Oh, just great – 'tarred and feathered' now, too.

I heard Trinity squealing and thrashing in the laundry in response to Spice's bark. "This is going to be a long month, isn't it?" I sighed.

Spice wasn't listening; she was already asleep.

I went into the next bedroom and slipped beneath the covers of the queen bed. Cotton sheets this time, with a silky doona that slid to the floor as soon as I moved around. I pulled it back up and right up to my chin, causing a large waft of air that brought with it another tarring-and-feathering experience. I closed my furry eyes for a moment. I was exhausted.

I could hear what sounded like owls hooting and calling, continuously, directly outside my window.

"I thought the country was supposed to be PEACEFUL and QUIET?" I muttered yet another rhetorical question to myself. My dreamy farm experience was so far anything but.

*****

The next day didn't start out any better. First thing in the morning I looked into the bathroom mirror and saw on my face not only remnants of Dalmatian hair, but book ink too. I had resorted to reading after accepting that the owls were going to serenade me all night, before I fell asleep mid-page in spite of them. The print from my book was all over my face. Each word was nearly legible, but unfortunately not water-soluble too.

"Must have fallen asleep and dribbled on my book…" I said lamely to the neighbour when he popped over unexpectedly after morning coffee to introduce himself.

"Rough night then, I take it?" Gary-the-neighbour gestured to the sleeping 'angels' under the kitchen table.

"If I agreed with you we would both be wrong!" I replied, with my best perky expression.

*****

In the afternoon I fed the now-awake-and-begging angels, then set myself to thoroughly cleaning the open fireplace. No sooner had I sat down to a well-deserved rest and tea break in the kitchen than there came ominously from the direction of the lounge room a thud, a squeal, and a large metallic bang. These were closely followed by the sounds of cat-cries and scuttling feet.

I was on my own feet by now and went bursting into the lounge room. I was greeted by the sight of Trinity covered in ash, the white couch decorated with little ashy kitty paw prints, and Spice all dusty with ash too. Unfortunately there was even more ash, as a plume in the air, but rapidly coming to settle EVERYWHERE. I could easily deduce that

Trinity had jumped or fallen into my ash bucket and scared Spice half to death; unfortunately my sudden appearance was the final straw and now they both bolted in fright straight out the back door and towards the hen house.

> *Don't let Trinity out of the house, she is an inside cat. And don't let Spice near the hens – she has a history of trapping them and biting their heads off.*

These final and DOUBLE-underlined sentences of Amity and Mika's letter flashed alarmingly in my mind as I heard the combination of awful sounds of squawking, flapping, and barking coming from outside.
"NOOOOOOOO!" I screamed, as I ran out the back door. How much worse could this get?

*****

The Strawberry Shortcake doll looked out of place in the paddock. I bent down and picked it up, then nervously scanned the area for whatever was making the new calf moo so much.

> *The cows will moo continually if a fox comes around. Call our friendly neighbour next door, number below, if you see any foxes.*

No visible foxes here, yet I called Gary to come back over anyway – with everything else that was going horribly wrong, I wasn't risking losing the new calf too.
I stood outside the paddock beside the gate and stroked the rag doll while I waited for Gary. The doll's little polka-dot bonnet was neatly sitting on her head, but her white pinafore was now not so white. She was still delightfully scented with a fresh fruity strawberry aroma. Someone was missing cuddling up to her at bedtime, no doubt. I noticed some of her hair – the red yarn – was all tatty. What was she doing here?

In the spruce tree near me sat a barn owl, wide awake, too early. It looked intently at me.

"Creepy!" I choked to myself under my breath. The owl hooted back to me, and continued to stare at me, unblinking, as though it understood. I was sure I saw some of the doll's red yarn hair wrapped around its talons as it sat there on the branch, still as a statue.

I saw Gary coming towards me, waving. That got the calf's attention too, and it decided to come closer to the fence as Gary approached. I waved back to Gary and then bent down to pick a daffodil from under the fence, thinking that this was such a pretty time of year. The calf gave a little moo and sniffed at my soon-to-be-picked daffodil; its mother had come closer to observe, too. Then BANG, I was flung backwards in one direction, and the calf went flying backwards in the opposite direction. I was aware of Gary running and shouting at me before I passed out.

*****

"That damn electric fence! Mika was supposed to turn it off before he left," apologised Amity from down the phone.

Gary had settled me on the ashy once-white couch, so that now I was lying as comfortably as I could considering that I was bleeding from my head (onto the couch, of course). Spice and Trinity watched on.

The house was starting to smell like festering death. Had an animal come inside to die? I could hear an owl, and saw one looking at me through the lounge room window. "What's with all the owls here always watching everything, Gary?" I asked irritably.

Amity and Mika hurried in the front door just at that moment.

"Who are you talking to?" asked Amity. "Who's Gary? And oh, where did you find that Strawberry Shortcake doll? I lost that when I was a child when the farm was my grandmother's!"

An owl flew in through the front door behind them, with red yarn hanging from its claw.

7. The Longest Nose on the Planet.

The woman, a psychiatrist, wore an expensive suit. She sat opposite me and put a photograph on the low table that separated us.

"Do you recognise these people?" she asked. She glared at me with her deep angry eyes.

The photo showed a woman, a young girl, a little dog, and the ocean; a delightful scene, with the people enjoying ice creams.

I smiled with familiarity, then frowned with the memories. I shook my head, then stared blankly.

"This is not your dog, this is not your summer trip, this is not your ice cream, and this is not your sunset." The woman in the expensive suit jabbed her fingertip on the photo each time she spoke, and also clicked a pen that she held in her other hand.

*****

That woman, the psychiatrist, was my mother. Now 20 years had passed and she was 20 years older. She was dressed in drab 'old lady' clothing, and sitting opposite me again. She handed me the same photo.

"Do you recognise these people?" she asked.

Same question, same tone, same gestures; the only thing that was different was me. But I responded in the same way. I smiled, then frowned, and shook my head, and stared.

My mother got the desired reaction she wanted, and walked away.

I tore up the photo. Satisfyingly, and slowly, shred by shred. I smiled a genuine smile – this would never be happening again.

Poor Mother. Dementia had claimed her wellbeing, and now she was simply on repeat.

As for Father, he'd had such outlandish ways. He only had opinions, all for himself. And if other people didn't match up to his expectations, then well, they were IN IT.

I was in it from my birth, apparently.

"The girl with the longest nose on the planet," fell on repeat from my father's oversized lips.

As the years went on, my proboscis increasingly became a bigger problem for both of them. "Take a photo, Maurine, and show her, just show her what she looks like, for heaven's sake!" my father would instruct my mother. And she obeyed, every time. "Take her to your office, Maurine," he would add, "and change her brain, fix all her issues, make her perfect! You seem to be able to do that with your other patients."

So these were the echoes I heard over the years, all the way up until Father died and Mother's brain shut down.

These days I understood that Munchausen syndrome by proxy existed. But before that, all my medical problems had been a 'normal' part of life. *She's just a sick girl.*

The condition was where the caretaker of a child, most often a mother, either made up fake illnesses, or caused the object of their care to become sick, or both. Back then, no one knew of Mother's mental problems and her abuse of me; she presented as the most dedicated and caring mother a child could ever need or want. But I had had so very many unnecessary surgeries over the years, with Mother spending countless hours in bedside vigil for me. Then as soon as I would make a recovery and try to recommence my life, reconnect with my school and friends, it was back to the photo inquisition, and my next major medical problem, and eventually the obsession with 'fixing this proboscis issue'.

"Just look at you, so happy and almost pretty on our beach holiday, enjoying your sunset ice cream. Don't you think it's such a shame that your nose is like that, dragging itself in the ice cream?"

I watched my mother disappear back through the security door, her nurse escorting her. The nurse waved to me and called, "See you next week! She does enjoy your visits."

I smiled, then frowned, and shook my head, and stared...and then I left the care home for the last time.

*****

I thought, *And here we fucking go again.*

But no, I meant, *Good morning!*

I stared past my steaming coffee cup, gazing out of my kitchen window. My mind wandered. I listened to my father's long-gone voice that nevertheless still sometimes rattled around in my head. There he was, down the years, first telling me that I had the longest nose on the planet. And at that very moment, at the age of six, I had felt myself dying...

I shook the thought clear, and sipped my coffee. It really was a delicious brew, and I should try to appreciate it. I sighed.

I reached up and scratched the cartilage that was protruding from the place where my nose would have been, if I still had a nose at all.

I was so BOTCHED.

How on earth did I get from there to here? I had another surgery scheduled for tomorrow. I was so SICK of nose surgeries. Why did I ever start?

Oh, yes... Mother. That's why.

Recently I had seen on the news that a girl in the USA was released from prison, where she had been serving a term of incarceration after killing her mother who had subjected her to Munchausen's by proxy.

I felt like I totally understood; I admit I had thought about it myself for years.

I knew one thing for sure – that saying to someone, "You're ugly!" was NOT a constructive approach.

Should a parent call a child ugly in order to be truthful, and 'help' the child to develop other skills and appreciate themselves for something else besides their actual 'faulty' feature? No! Never! Not! Ever!

Why on earth would a parent intentionally, knowingly, tear their child down? For what purpose? My astonished friends would ask me this. No, they were not just astonished – they were incredulous. Time and again, the same questions. What are they actually hoping to teach that child by doing that? *Are they imbeciles?*

I knew that it was a parent's job, their DUTY, to build their children up. To lift them up with praise for a job well done. To encourage them. To stack layer upon layer of self-confidence on them. To not only TELL them how proud they made their parents, but to SHOW them with love, touch, and positive facial expressions. And to tell friends and family how great the child was, and to do this *in front of the child.* To give the child a sense of accomplishment. To teach them that they can do anything if they try. That it's okay to fail as long as you get back up on your feet; get back up on your feet and try again and again if it's something you truly want. A parent should do all of these things, wanting and hoping to build a well-rounded, confident, intelligent, relatively happy, strong in mind, driven and capable adult. One who is able to deal with life, make good decisions, be employable, know how to love others, and more. An adult who can and will survive, and thrive, because the parent of the child taught and gave them what they needed to be a capable human being, with the ability to take care of themselves, take care of situations, take care of others, and do whatever they want to do in their life. All because the parent built the child up with positive feedback, positive strokes, and positive intentions, and did it with love.

Give this child nurture and self-love, not degradation and self-loathing! A child's life could crumple into a heap on the floor because their parents did not do their job properly as parents. I felt that I could speak with some authority on what parents should do, having had such experience of what parents should NOT do. I recalled my cousin praising me, not too long ago, saying how surprised and grateful she was that I had 'turned out all okay' and wasn't 'psycho' after all that had happened to me. No, I was not one who had crumpled. In spite of everything.

*****

"That child of yours became exactly what you wanted and hoped she would be! Job well done!" Mother's friends had often said to her. They were so sympathetic to her plight, and in awe of how devoted she was to her chronically sick child, and admiring of how she had helped me achieve the milestones of growing up, seemingly against all odds. And Mother had lapped it all up.

There was a gorgeous photo that was taken at my high school graduation. Mother made sure that I (and she) didn't miss 'occasions' – somehow they were always worked around my hospital visits and my home convalescences. Or perhaps vice versa. Mother always made such a fuss over my outfits, which she chose herself, and my hair, which she refused to let anyone but herself cut or style.

I had heard Mother say, "Oh, look, Roger, she looks divine, doesn't she? I love her hair that way, don't you?"

I heard her, and I was hungry for positivity, and I was almost touched. But as always, if it wasn't one of them, it was the other.

"You can't dress up ugly, Maurine!" Father snorted. This time I pretended that I didn't hear.

I think that was the day I started researching plastic surgery.

As a child and well into my teenage years, whenever I was taken to the zoo I would go and sit in front of the monkey cages and watch them play, and live, and interact, and communicate. One large cage held several individuals of *Nasalis larvatus*, commonly known as the proboscis monkey, or long-nosed monkey, native to the mangrove forests and coastal areas of Borneo. I would stare at them for hours. One older male monkey would often come up and sit, on the other side of the bars, immediately across from me. His little fingers were wrapped around the hard wire of the cage, and he would stare back at me.

"I know how you feel, mate," I whispered.

I felt like I belonged with them. Especially with my little friend directly on the other side of the bars. My nose was practically identical to his, and I was okay with him looking at me. One time I could even joke, "I think mine is longer than yours!" He had chattered and gestured, as if he knew exactly what I had said. I felt like we understood each other perfectly. The monkeys were the only ones who could talk about my nose and I wouldn't feel bad about it.

But my father... I continued to despise my father's obsession with my nose, that had made me obsessed as well. I noticed more and more that other people looked at me too, and pointed at me, and I hated it. Mostly I hated being Father's crazy sideshow and joke punching bag.

"Roger, just leave it alone, would you?" I would hear Mother shout sometimes, as she and my father argued loudly in the upstairs bedroom. "It's only a nose! You will make her paranoid, and we have much bigger fish to fry, what with all her medical issues!"

Mother would sob then, and when I was very young and naïve I thought she was defending me, instead of just trying to assert her rights to be the one to fully control me.

Father would continue attacking my appearance, always finding new insults. One time it was, "When she lies down she makes a good sundial,

Maurine!" And another time, "Who knew that Walt Disney was to be inspired by it?"

Eventually, Mother stopped fighting Father about my nose, and started to agree with him. With my adult wisdom, I'm actually surprised it took her as long as it did to 'switch' her side, because once she did, he no longer argued with her, and she now had all the means to exercise complete dominion over me. She made the most of it.

Sometimes I don't know how I survived it all, and I so easily could have gone 'psycho', as my cousin had feared I would. I truly think that it was only because the zoo had become my safe space, a place to escape, from both of them, and find some shred of sanity, that I was able to hold on long enough and not implode. The zoo was all I had, until I could find the strength to actually get out from Mother's control. Or until fate could help me.

*****

Soon after my first botched nose surgery, Father died.

Mother died inside, that day, when he never came home. I had come back from a depressing post-surgical check to find her sobbing on the kitchen floor. She acted like she didn't even recognise me, and for the first time in my life she shut herself away from me and left me completely to my own devices. And continued to do so, for several months. Somehow I found myself able to function as an independent person. I took myself to the zoo and told my special monkey friend that I was working on being free. He was the only one who didn't stare at my face.

Father had hated my nose, and had probably hated me, but he still left all of his money to me in his will. And I knew what I wanted to do with it, what I had wanted for years, but that had been only a dream.

I had come a long way, and I made my dream come true. I purchased the zoo's café and moved into the one-bedroom apartment attached to it, the caretaker's unit. Now I could commune with the monkeys whenever I wanted, and I had found a proper home.

Months later, Mother was still lurking about her own home, a shadow of her former self. She missed my father, which both surprised and disgusted me. She would keep calling his phone so that she could hear his voicemail bank message over and over. Torturing herself, daily. The focus was off me, and I thought I was finally free, but I still couldn't leave it alone.
"Mother, why?" I asked. "Don't you think you need to let go?"
She turned wet eyes to me. "It's the nicest thing he ever said!"
Frig, how sad is that? I thought of him as a destroyer of lives.
But Mother continued to call his phone, and every time, his voicemail said: "Hey, this is your man Roger, I can't pick up right now because I'm taking my gorgeous wife out to lunch. But you know what to do, over and out!"
He had never taken her out for any meal, EVER.

It was not much after that that she almost burned her house down. I never knew if it was an accident or not; I don't think even she could say for sure which it was. But that was when she had started living in the dementia care home. And reverted to her psychiatrist persona ritual whenever I visited. I never asked the nurses what she did when I wasn't visiting. I just wasn't interested.

*****

I had returned to the zoo, the only place I felt at home, and at ease. Periodically I had visited Mother, and periodically I had submitted to yet another nose surgery, each one seemingly less successful than the last. My patterns fell into years. My special monkey friends and I all got older, but we all still understood one other.

One day I moved from the monkeys to the elephants, and sat and watched them for a while, marvelling at what an imposing and majestic sight they were. Absolutely magical behemoths with amazing proboscises! My father was totally wrong, and so was I – it was the elephants who had the longest noses on the planet. Suddenly I was looking at a large nose, not with loathing, but with admiration at the advantage it was. For the elephant, not a burden of ugliness, but a truly unique and important multi-purpose blessing to an incredible creature.

I sat, unmoving and thinking, on the bench seat for hours, even while rain steadily fell. I was over 30 kilograms heavier than I needed to be, but comfortable in my own skin for the first time in my 40 years. I would NOT be doing anything about my weight, as every so-called well-meaning friend was telling me to – external advice in some ways could be a bigger burden than my old 'ugly' derisions.

I reflected that the nose thing hadn't turned out so well for me, but with my new enlightenment, I thought that maybe that was wrong too, and perhaps things had actually turned out exactly as they were supposed to for me.

As I sat there soaking, a distinguished-looking man came along who was also drenched – so much so that I heard his boots squelching as he walked up and sat on the wettest part of the bench, right next to me.

"Beautiful day," he remarked, with a broad smile.

I looked sideways at him twice, trying to figure out if he was actually talking to me, or just to himself.

"Beautiful day!" he repeated. "Sunshine will be out soon, also beautiful, just like you."

I couldn't choke out even a hello.

"Um, thank you..." I finally managed to whisper.

Um, thank you was all I could say! I was looking right at him now, and seeing him looking straight past my disfigured face and deep into my eyes and my soul.

"You have such a sparkle and clarity about you," he continued.

"I...I do?" I asked, as my jaw dropped and wouldn't shut.

He handed me a towel, one that matched a second towel he kept hold of. They were both as wet as each other.

"Here," he said, shooting me another smile, "let me buy you a nice hot cup of coffee. Let's go."

I finally managed to close my mouth. He stood and took my hand and pulled me to my feet, and then we walked and made small talk as we went to the zoo café. We grabbed coffees and sat in a well-lit corner, in a booth seat at the back. He seemed very at home in that exact spot.

"I'll lay it all out," he began. "Welcome to my home. I live here at the zoo; I actually own these zoological gardens. I've seen you often over the years, and I have just now plucked up the courage to meet you. In the rain." He smiled broadly again.

I couldn't resist that grin, and that honesty. We chatted and giggled and dried off. Then he had to go, but we made plans to meet up the next day. And when we said goodbye, he put his arms around me and we hugged, and I instantly felt warm and safe and loved. And content.

So, in my mind, I officially had the longest nose on the planet, and now probably the most botched nose on the planet, too. But finally, it didn't matter. I no longer cared if people judged me. The important thing was that I had stopped judging myself, and no more of my soul was left unhealed.

My favourite author, Joanna Gaines, had written, "Don't quit, and don't give up, either. The reward is just around the corner."

Don't give up, don't ever give up. Because sometimes, the reward is 40 years in the making, and it comes to you when and where and how you least expect it. Even in the rain, beside the elephant enclosure.

8. The Intelligent Energy.

I didn't know what had come together in my cup as I looked down into my Stone Street coffee, but whatever it was, I was balancing it all, and deliciously! The thrill of moving hadn't yet worn off. I couldn't imagine it ever would.

It certainly had me not wanting to go into the office…

I was so excited at finally having bought a place of my own. I came from 'old money' and people might assume I would have purchased something grand for myself long ago. But I was making my way in the world with a little more independence than some in my family (I actually had a job, for one…) and was more frugal in some things than many of my relatives could ever hope to understand. Of course the places I looked at were bound to be expensive, but I still had sticker shock, again and again!

I had been looking just long enough to have had to struggle to find exactly the right place for me. I wanted a single-family home, but with today's market and my own particular standards of value for money, plus availability in New York City, it seemed that nothing would give me everything I wanted.

The one thing that was absolutely a must was my own pool. And then suddenly, there it was – 509 Pacific, as the ONLY property with a backyard pool. A truly unique home.

I couldn't be happier that it was now mine.

I had moved in and settled myself. That first night I'd had a few glasses of champagne around the pool, and the next day I had ordered a new designer patio suite. I was set!

I felt fortunate the seller had offered me most of the household furniture that already filled the four-story home. I had taken it, of course – it was beautiful and stylish. There was all manner of gorgeous art, and a stocked library, too (too good to be true!). I couldn't believe it, though I was glad, that the seller wished to keep none of the books – there were so many of them it would probably take me years to read them all.

The seller, not operating through a realtor, had impressed me with his generosity with the house and its contents. I was also quietly appreciative of his good looks, and his easy personality.

I was surprised, but extremely pleased, when he asked me out on a date. BONUS!

Our first date went well. We had decided on brunch in a little hidden bistro nearby. The food was wonderful, and I thanked him for showing me this place – I doubted I would have found it on my own until much later. What a waste of feast opportunity that would have been! He smiled at that, and said he knew the area well, but he hadn't lived at the property. We chatted naturally, we giggled, then we dined some more, and we ended up staying at the bistro until late into the afternoon. Afterwards he came back to the house for a drink, and we chatted some more.

I suggested a sunset swim. Ashton declined, with a wince that he couldn't quite hide. I thought that maybe he wasn't a water person.

"I'll just sit here and watch the moon go overhead, if that's all right by you," he said, taking my hand across the table.

I wasn't going to object! *What a catch, is he for real?*
Suddenly, I felt like I had made it.

I wondered, how do you know when you have reached your goals and dreams? To me, it was more than merely ticking the boxes, though I've ticked most of them anyway. But sometimes, the energy behind success feels like there is MORE.

I looked forward to getting to know my new home, and new…friends. I felt that 509 Pacific was my dream home. It felt like my home had secrets it was waiting to tell me. I didn't know the history of the house, but I was sure its walls would talk to me, if I was quiet and listened with respect. I could tell the place had been well loved, and also had been renovated from its original three-story structure, as it had passed through its various owners' hands. I was looking forward to making my own changes, in due course. Some of the décor was a little skewed from my taste – that marble Appaloosa horse statue in the entryway would have to go, for one thing – but there was time enough for culling the things that didn't work for me and adding to the place with things that did. This was going to be my forever home, so I could afford a leisurely redesign.

*****

In the library, with my feet up on one arm of the couch I was lying on, I turned the last page and put the book down on the coffee table. I sighed. This was a milestone.

It had indeed taken years to get through the library contents – almost five, to be precise. And now there was just one small shelf of books left to read. It would be the end of an era when I was done with them.

Five years in this house had had its ups and downs. Mostly ups, but the downs had been pretty intense. Sadly, my relationship with Ashton was ultimately a down – it had not lasted. It was sad, and a little bizarre. The trouble had started when I had had my tripping accident.

A few weeks into my life in my new home, I had started to think I was going mad. One night, from my top-story bedroom suite, I could have sworn I saw someone swimming in my pool.

"Hey!" I shouted out of my window. "Hey, YOU!"

The person just floated, ignoring my shouting.

"Oh, hell no!" I muttered, incensed that some ASSHOLE was swimming in MY precious pool. "Oh no you don't!"

I heard a splash, and took off running in fury, racing down the stairs, my heart pounding. I took the stairs two at a time, almost losing my footing more than once, but somehow making it down safely. I passed the floor-to-ceiling window overlooking the pool area, and I could see the dark silhouette of the trespasser in the deep end of the pool.

I raced out into the pool area…and tripped violently over my new patio furniture. I hit the deck face-first with a sickening smack. When I had sat up in a daze, the pool invader was nowhere to be seen. I held my swollen and bleeding lip as I looked back and forth – no intruder, and no wet footprints on the deck, either.

I fetched an ice pack from the kitchen and retreated back to my bedroom, feeling very sorry for myself.

I heard splashing! And again, from my window, I saw the shadow in the pool.

I raced down the stairs again, and this time I wasn't so lucky. This time I did lose my footing, halfway down, and I hit my forehead when I fell. But I had learned my lesson. I called the police, who also called a paramedic to assess my injuries. It was decided I didn't need to go to the hospital, or the police station. The police didn't find the intruder. And the intruder didn't come back.

When I told Ashton about the whole incident, he was sympathetic about my injuries, but didn't seem that interested in hearing about the trespasser in my pool. From that day onwards, though, he started to act a little strangely around me.

Sometimes when he was visiting me, he seemed to be a little jumpy, looking over his shoulder, avoiding looking in mirrors, and secretly inspecting the pool from every vantage point in the house. In all honesty, I thought it was a little ridiculous that he had suddenly seemed to become more worried about trespassers than I was!

When I overheard him muttering to himself in the library, and I thought I made out the name 'Amelia', I couldn't help but confront him. As soon as I did, and mentioned the name of Amelia, he dropped heavily onto the couch and covered his face with his hands.

"My former fiancée," he said, in a muffled voice.

"WHAT?" I said. I was stunned. We hadn't been dating that long, and hadn't really delved into each other's pasts, but I thought the fact that he had once been engaged might have warranted a casual sentence or two, at the very least.

"I don't want to talk about it!" he shouted, suddenly jumping up. "It's over, it's done with! The end!"

He stormed out.

Stupidly, I felt jealous. I tried Googling, but of course only a reasonably common first name wasn't enough to find anything. I could see nothing about her on Ashton's social media, either; though perhaps, given what I had just witnessed, that wasn't surprising.

It took Ashton three days to come back. I had a million questions, but I asked none of them.

For the next couple of weeks, we tried to continue as if nothing had happened. But he was still tiptoeing around the house, and poking here and there when he thought I wasn't watching him. Finally, when I saw him picking the leaves off the Virginia creeper by the kitchen window trellis, I couldn't help but ask, "What are you doing? Are you looking for something in particular?"

He looked like a kid who'd been caught with his hand in the cookie jar. "No," he responded, "I just get paranoid sometimes."

"Of what?" I asked. "And why?"

His expression changed, and his chin came up. "I get anxious sometimes. Especially HERE." He looked hard at me. And then he *sneered*.

My jaw dropped. "Are you blowing me off?" I attacked, wide-eyed.

"Maybe it's YOU that's paranoid!" he fired back.

That stung, because I *was* on edge, because of HIM, so how dare he turn it back on me? And that was it – I didn't need this crap.

"I don't need this crap!" I spat my thoughts out loud. "This is MY life and this is MY home – GET OUT!" And just to sting him in return, I added viciously, "Just go back to Amelia!"

He went pale and then glared at me.

I practically shoved him out the door.

Another relationship gone.

And now it was nearly five years later. I hadn't heard from or seen Ashton since. Sometimes I thought I missed him. Yes, that whole episode was definitely a down.

*****

I dispensed with my depressing five-year-old memories, and shook the cobwebs of the past out of my head.

I tried to relax. Perhaps I would start a book from the last shelf.

I picked out a thin, well-worn volume with a gray cover.

It was called 'Awaken From Death', by Emanuel Swedenborg. With a title like that, it didn't seem like it would be a relaxing read, so I only half-heartedly flicked it open. I saw immediately that it was annotated with handwritten notes, and many passages were highlighted or circled.

At first I was more curious about the notes than the book itself. I wondered if I would get an insight into the previous owner of the book (or perhaps owners, plural, as it appeared that there were two different styles of handwriting represented), and therefore of the house. But as I read the notes, especially in context of the book, I began to become interested by the concept of the book itself. Its blurb read 'A detailed description of the soul's journey into the spiritual realm upon bodily death' and in spite of my initial misgivings, I was fascinated by this. As I read on and on, I found myself comforted by Swedenborg's ideas of souls as intelligent energies, and intrigued by the questions and comments in the handwritten notes. I wondered if it could possibly be true, that there was a continuation of self after death. A part of me really wanted to think that it was.

The book was not long, and even with reading all the annotations as well, I soon reached the end. And made another 'interesting' discovery.

Inside the back cover were taped two photographs.

The first, an older faded one, was of a small boy, sitting on an Appaloosa horse (a real one, not the entryway statue that for some reason I kept putting off getting rid of). The bridle of the horse was being held by a woman. She was smiling, and so was the little boy. I lifted the photo, which was only taped at the top, to read on the reverse: 'My Ashton, age 6, and his proud mother.' I gasped. And I was sure this was the same handwriting as the majority of the notations in the book itself.

I was still processing the implications of the first picture when my eye was drawn to the second photograph, taped underneath the first one, and revealed properly by my having lifted the first photograph. The second picture was of Ashton as a grown man, perhaps a few years younger than the Ashton I had briefly dated. He was standing next to a beautiful young brunette woman. They were dressed formally, and they were smiling. I recognized my grand reception room, and saw what were clearly party guests, out of focus in the background of the picture. My eyes returned to study the brunette. She had her right hand tucked through Ashton's arm, but she was holding her left hand out to the camera, to show off the large diamond sparkling on her ring finger. On the reverse of this picture was more handwriting, and this time it matched with the second, smaller lot of notes in the book. The second photo's caption read: 'For Mother – wish you could have been here. Home is not the same without you.'

"What the FUCK?" I exclaimed. So, this was Ashton's MOTHER'S house? How dare he not tell me! He had let me believe that he had just inherited the house from a *distant* relative and had offered it for sale immediately. I was so angry. But I thought it at least explained his weird behavior when he would visit me here, all his poking around...was he looking for memories of his mother? And wait...when we were dating, had he been coming here for me, or for *her?*

Now I was absolutely FURIOUS. I wanted to know more. I still had Ashton's number in my phone (stupid, I know, after five years...), but when I tried calling it, it was disconnected.

I desperately NEEDED to know MORE! I looked at the little shelf again – perhaps there were more books, notes, photographs...

My eye was immediately caught by an orange spine, and the fact I could see a bookmark sticking out of the middle of the book. I snatched up the book, called 'A Clue to the Invisible Pyramid', and quickly flipped through it. It was much newer than the Swedenborg book, and did not have any notes or photographs inside. Just the bookmark, at page 115, marking the start of a very short story.

My eyes opened wide as I read it...

509 PACIFIC

That was a wonderful summer of so many amazing memories. The house was built next to my childhood home. I never thought I would go back to the same neighborhood that I grew up in, but 509 Pacific is the most magical home I've ever lived in. It's not a typical New York apartment, for one main reason – it has a pool. I'm not aware of any other New York CBD home that has an outdoor pool in its own garden space.

Built in magnificent Petersen brick, my home combined sophistication and superior craftsmanship in the heart of Boerum Hill. My four-story condominium home is all about space, volume and massive proportions. My son once brought over his new girlfriend and their two friends. I instantly didn't like the pair of friends; he resembled a thug and she resembled a call girl (I didn't catch their actual names, but as far as I was concerned, I had named them!). They all got tipsy on my imported Champagne, smashed the wet bar on my rooftop space, then wanted to go for a swim. I certainly put a stop to it all, frustratedly asked them all to leave, and gave my son a big frown as they departed. "If you ever want to sell, we'll buy it!" slurred Harlot, as she stumbled and tripped down my front steps.

The summer came and went. I enjoyed many a sunset on the roof, soaking in the tub looking out over the Brooklyn skyline and its twinkling lights, and floating around in my little historic and rare pool. The winter was particularly cold, and the snow came for nearly the entire time between October and May, very unseasonable with intense blizzards, but it turns out I can hardly recall ANY of the winter now, as I float around in my pool blissfully. It seems all my memories have been deleted from my brain, from December onwards. I don't recall Christmas, or the holidays at all; must have been boring. The summer had definitely arrived though, and all I wanted to do was float around in my pool. I'm so lucky to have had the opportunity to retire and now just float – float for eternity looking up at the full moon, high in the daytime sky.

I watch the moon pass over the rooftops and skyline and pop out the other side. I've lost track of time as I float. I hear some noises, and giggling, and the clinking of glasses. Four people walk through my patio door and place their goodies on my sundeck chairs, place MY imported bottles of Champagne on the side tables. "HEY, HEY!" I shout at them, but they just ignore me. "ASHTON! WHAT ON EARTH?" I shout at my son and his awful friends. "I'll call the police!"

To my disgust, Harlot then strips completely naked under the failing light, and joins me in the pool.

"OH NO, NO YOU DONT!" I go up and splash her. My splashing doesn't deter her – she doesn't react at all, and I think she must already be very drunk (she had better not throw up in my pool...).

"Your mother would be missing this – it's so magical here, Ash," spits out Harlot.

"Gross, Delilah!" Thug shouts to her. "That's the same water she died in!" As if realizing a possible insensitivity, Thug continues, "So sorry for your loss again, Ash, but glad you let us move in with you. You need your friends right now, even though I think your mother would hate us being here all the time – she's probably turning in her grave..."

I continue to stare at them in silence, as they splash and shout, not reacting to me at all. Now I can make neither splash nor ripple in the pool. Harlot floats and floats, always naked, and always too close to me.

I felt dazed. I didn't understand. Or rather, I did, but I didn't want to. Something stirred in my memory, something from years ago. I seemed to recall reports of a woman who had drowned in her pool, and her son didn't find her until three days later...bloated, floating...floating...

Shit! That was here, in THIS house?

Damn it, I was totally creeped out now. I needed to get out of the library, and I most DEFINITELY needed a drink! I turned and left the room, and started to run down the stairs, thinking I would drink my lower bar dry, with the way I was feeling.

I lost my footing on the stairs, for the first time in five years, like an idiot, and actually somersaulted down the last few steps. I bumped my head and my shoulder but it was my butt that felt really bruised, even more so than my pride. I picked myself up and staggered to the bar and swigged directly out of the closest open bottle, without even tasting what it was, just appreciating the burning in my throat.

I leaned against the bar and finished the bottle. Then I grabbed another one. I practically crawled back up the stairs, clutching a third bottle. I fell into bed and drank myself into oblivion.

When I woke it was the late afternoon. I felt very sore and sorry for myself, though how much was due to my tumble and how much to my hangover, I couldn't say. I spent the remainder of the day in bed, falling asleep again in the early evening, and the next time I woke it was morning. Time to actually get out of bed, perhaps. I didn't know when I had last had so much sleep, but at least my head felt clearer.

I checked my phone and was surprised to see no missed messages or calls. Well, perhaps that was why I was able to sleep for so long. On a sour note, it seemed that my power was out – neither the lights nor the cable TV were working. I would have to check my fuse box and hope that it was an easy fix I could handle myself – I wasn't in the mood to have to deal with electricians or the power company.

I headed downstairs, trying to remember if I actually had any spare fuses, and where they would even be. I didn't get very far to wondering, because I saw a figure walk past my kitchen window. It looked like Ashton! I called out to him and knocked on the window. He ignored me and kept walking, so I ran to the side bay window and called again to him from there. He walked faster. I was more than angry now – what did he think he was doing?

I went outside, ready to give him a piece of my mind. Where had he gone? I heard splashing, coming from my pool. *Oh hell no, not again!* He was clearly insane! He was going to be sorry he was messing with me.

I heard more splashing, then *singing,* and clinking of glasses. I rounded the corner to the pool deck, ready with shouting.

I stopped dead at what I saw.

Ashton was in my pool, all right, and he wasn't alone. There were at least a half a dozen other people in there, too, all merrily splashing, floating, drinking, enjoying themselves.

"WHAT THE HELL IS GOING ON?" I found my voice, screaming. I was trembling, *shaking.* This was crazy! I felt like *I* was going crazy!

"About time you came to join us," smiled Ashton, as if he had not just ignored me calling him. And as if we had last parted as friends yesterday instead of acrimoniously five years before.

"What the hell are you doing?" I shrieked. "You can't be here, you can't swim in my pool, you can't have glass in my pool, you can't invite strangers into MY POOL! I'm calling the police and getting all your asses arrested – even you, Ashton!"

My blood was really boiling now.

"Calm down," replied Ashton, still smiling. "We're all friends, here, now. And family, of course."

For the first time, I looked properly at the other people in the pool. And I recognized a couple of them. And I did calm down, because I froze, and just stared. My brain felt like it could not take in the information being presented to me.

Amelia was smiling at me now, too. "A bit shocking, I know," she said. "But it's all good, you'll see. I will pour you a glass of bubbly; we have to celebrate! Because I really do have to thank you for telling Ashton to come back to me. You made him realize there was no point at all in living without me, so he managed to find his way to me."

"Definitely cause for celebration!" nodded Ashton's mother, and she was smiling as well. "In fact I've been celebrating Ashton and Amelia for a little while now, the way I never got to do before."

I found that I was standing in the shallow end of the pool, but I couldn't recall how I got there.

"I don't…I don't understand…" I murmured.

"I think you do," said Ashton's mother, very gently. "Didn't you get the memo?"

I frowned. Ashton's mother answered my unspoken question.

"Yes, the blue highlighter mark in our book," said the intelligent energy, "on page 11. Where I also wrote in my red pen when I was still alive, 'I hope I get to spend eternity having a party with my friends and family, in my pool in my forever home'."

She beamed at me.

I looked down at myself, standing in the pool. I moved my hand through the water. The water did not move at all.

I raised my head and shook it slowly, then looked at them all in turn, searching for help.

The Amelia intelligent energy smiled at me again, and smiled at Ashton beside her, holding her hand.

Ashton's mother said to me, "It's all right, really. I couldn't always move the water either, at first, or anything else! But you'll be fine, you'll get there. It just takes practice." She smiled at me again, reassuringly. "And there's plenty of time."

Upstairs in the library, lying on the sofa, was the Swedenborg book, open at page 11. There were red-penned notes in the margins, and the blue highlighter marked the first line of the second paragraph.

> *I have often heard that people who arrived from the world were delighted to see their friends again, and that their friends were delighted in turn at their arrival.*

*****

The new 'FOR SALE' sign attached to the brick façade read, in part:

This luxurious condominium retains its classical details, including its unique original pool.

9. The Terra Experiment.

Waking before my alarm, again.

Surviving the night, again.

Awakening from an awesome dream of living blissfully way up in the mountains, but now realizing that I'm just existing.

PTSD will do that.

But it's not just that. I'm stale, like one of Grannie's cakes that sat for a while. Tasteless, unattractive, dry and lackluster.

Yet still in existence.

*****

My enlistment was to ignite my sense of adventure and giving back to my country, but how wrong I was. I was a retired veteran at 33.

I sank into my mother's couch, my brown outfit matching the color of the upholstery. If not for the white cushion I hugged, and Lilly, the family's black cat cuddled against my legs, I would be invisible.

I looked up at my father's recliner. It was empty, of course. I missed him, in spite of everything.

Parents are not perfect, but Mother nearly was.

My eyes closed. All I really wanted was to be able to sleep well again. I tried to focus. To consciously metamorphose my thoughts into something positive, as I had always done before when I closed my eyes.

Control.

Emmy-Lou Nieman, that was me.

I wasn't really sure why my parents named me Emmy-Lou. I think I would have preferred to be called something a bit less conspicuous. Like Tina, perhaps – I felt like that was more 'me', somehow. But Emmy-Lou I was, and so I just learned to live with it. But I also never understood hyphenating your kid's name; it was beyond me. No one else in my life had a hyphenated name until I made it to my teenage years, but before that I was robbed of happiness at elementary school. *Emmy-Lou-Does-A-Poo.* Kids can be really cruel.

I never felt like I belonged in my house either, because of my father. I was waiting for the day I would be informed that I was adopted. But it never came.

The best day of my life was being accepted into the military academy straight out of school, and I moved away after basic training. My military career was less than illustrious and far shorter than I had expected; quite disappointing really. My platoon had been hit by a Scud. I was the only survivor. I grieved intensely for those lost, and survivor's guilt found me hard. My intrusive thoughts declined my mood, and angry outbursts and helplessness overcame me. I moved back into my family home, but the noise and pace of the city, and a mother who didn't or couldn't understand me, left me in a holding pattern. "Well, you lived, Emmy-Lou," Mother would say. "Can't you be happy for yourself that you are at least alive and have a chance at life?" She just didn't get it.

Some days were full of malaise – convalescing, languishing, prostrate. On other days I could exercise, pick myself up, and function. On those days I hiked – being out in nature was blissfully serene and quiet, the only time and place I wasn't plagued with intense flashbacks.

I'd had a job immediately after retirement, but it didn't last. Neither did my relationship with my fiancé, which just left me more devastated. I was disappointed in myself for just how overwhelming my devastation was, and for a while I starved myself – it was the one thing that was still under my control.

"You're getting too skinny, Emmy-Lou," said my concerned sister Bess each time she visited. This was unhelpful, to say the least.

I sank further into the couch, under the watchful eye of the recliner. It was as if Father was still sitting there, judging. *Creepy.*

My post-military job had seemed like the answer initially, because I was determined to make a go of this civilian life. But it was over in a matter of days, courtesy of a proclamation from my boss: "Everything you do, every step you take, every conversation you have and every breath you draw needs to be all about your work, and never about your personal life, loves, or desires, get it?"

In that moment I had decided this wasn't for me. Who knew that animal control would require so much dedication? That motto sounded like something you would say to an assassin, not a civil servant. I had just wanted to work with animals. Animals are uncomplicated and a great distraction. I liked and needed uncomplicated and distracted. I knew some fun facts about goats. Four stomachs, rectangular eyes, they love paper, their scream sounds like a screaming child, they sneeze to warn each other when there's danger, and they know their names. I had always wanted goats. And I wanted land. I needed space, not a feeling of four walls caving in on me and an empty recliner that haunted me.

*****

I had never known precisely what I needed before, but now I did. So I did something about it, and then it all came to a head and out into the open after a conversation when Bess next came over to visit.

No one sat in Father's recliner. Bess sat next to me on the couch with Lilly between us stealing as many available pats as possible, and Mother sat in her new chair. We talked, awkwardly, as I tried to think how to share my news.

I don't even know how it came up, but suddenly I was hearing for the first time that my father had died trying to impress another woman, and in the event killing 33 other people too. I had had no idea. He was a boat captain; I had just thought he went to work and never came home. But that's when I had left too. I thought I left Mother and Bess grieving Father's death, but they had subsequently discovered a whole 25 years of Father trying to impress other women. Almost like a triple abandonment for my poor mother.

And now I was going to leave them again.

Mother had been horrified when I had quit my 'stable council job' but I had told her I would not be controlled. And now I knew I needed more freedom still, so just like that, I dropped my own bombshell.

"I bought my own place," I blurted out. "I'm moving up by the Canadian border, about five hours' drive from here."

My words were met with stunned expressions.

The silence lengthened, until I had to break it.

"It's a deceased estate property, rundown cabins, needs a lot of work, has woods, 100 acres of land, river and well water, out of the way of the nearest towns," I babbled. "I saw it for sale, and knew my military payout would cover it, with plenty left over. It sounded perfect; I jumped at it. I'll live in my van while I work to get the cabins habitable."

I didn't tell them that I hadn't even seen photos of the place yet.

Bess finally spoke. "We really need to all stick together, Em," she said quietly. "For Mother."

"I'm sorry, Bess," I replied, just as quietly. "I can't stick to anything, not right now. Let me sort myself out. I'll make it up to you."

Mother still said nothing, but she put her head down. She had heard those words before.

I'll make it up to you.

*****

By the time the day came for me to leave for my new home, Mother had at least come around to the inevitable. After the morning ritual of 6.00 am coffee, she even packed some supplies for me – drink flasks, a five-pound bag of ground coffee, and a box of groceries. Mother and Bess and I hugged tightly. I told them I hoped they could visit soon. They told me they hoped that too.

I drove, and drove. My worn-out van rattled and I was sure a few screws and things fell off into the road along the way. "That's OK," I muttered to myself, "as long as the floor holds and my building supplies make it there intact." I was heading to a derelict property that I had purchased sight unseen, but I had no doubts that I was doing the right thing. 'Undiscovered paradise' had been the enticing opening words of the realty ad. It was a bargain, really, because the previous owner had actually perished on the property, and the sale had reflected that – the prime land alone was probably worth twice the asking price.
I couldn't wait to get there.

The five-hour drive north seemed like nothing compared to the winding trail that was the driveway on my new property (I had almost missed the hidden turn to it) – 'potholed' was the understatement of the century. The trail was a few miles long, and at one point I stopped to pick up the front fender of my van, that had me stuck in a rut, literally. But when I wasn't cursing the road, I was admiring my new home. I drove past old-growth apple trees, elders, cottonwoods and spruce. The river running through my land was truly amazing, with idyllic surrounds, like something you might see pictured in a hunting magazine.
When I finally reached the cabins I was glad to get out of the van and stretch my stiff legs. I wandered around happily, inspecting everything. The cabins themselves turned out to be very dilapidated. One was little more than a stone and timber ramshackle lean-to, while the other was not much better, just with a surprisingly new-looking chimney. But there was

a working well, a bunch more apple trees, a lot of unmaintained garden (containing copious root vegetables), and acres and acres of woods and fields all around.

I felt a magnetism, like I had homed in on something that could reenergize me.

It was heaven.

I closed my eyes and raised my face to the sun.

"Wow, she's a beauty, hey?" came a man's voice from behind me.

I jumped and spun around.

"Miz Emmy-Lou Neiman, I presume?" asked an older man in a sheriff's uniform, walking with a limp towards me. "I'm your welcoming party today. The realtor, Harry, isn't coming. He's actually my son. Kids, huh?" The sheriff smiled, but then nodded seriously to me, "I hope you've got a couple of guns, too; you might need them."

"Yes, I have my father's guns," I answered, like I was under suspicion, "and I have all the right paperwork."

"It's OK, Emmy-Lou," he chuckled at my wary expression, "and I'm sure you can use them well, given your previous profession."

Statement received as intended. I nodded.

"I've got this," I confirmed, and offered him my hand. "And please call me Em."

"I'm Bud, the local sheriff, at your service," he replied, shaking hands firmly. "No keys needed to hand over this purchase, huh?"

I smiled slightly at that.

"Pretty isolated out here," Bud added. "Town is 30 miles west, and I'm your closest neighbor at 20 miles east. You know?"

I nodded. "Recon."

"Of course," said Bud. "You got bear spray?"

I nodded again; I was well prepared there. I even had several of those new and very expensive pocket-sized canisters, but I didn't tell him that.

"You don't say much."

I nodded once more.

He handed me a card and I placed it in the leg pocket of my hunting pants. I walked into the bigger cabin, a roofless shack named 'Paradise'. Bud limped after me, rattling off some inaudible babble as he stood on what remained of the porch. I started to inspect my soon-to-be home.

Bud's voice became louder. "I said, Emmy-Lou, call me whenever you want – I'm here to help you. And do you want to know any details of how Big Red Dumfries died? You do know he died here, hey?"

"Em!" I shouted from inside. "Call me Em! And nope, no thanks, don't need any Big Red details."

"Well, if you're sure," said Bud, probably disappointed there was nothing more to talk about. "I guess I'll come back to check up on you in two weeks, see how you're doing. You living in your van until you do up the place?"

"Yup!" I shouted from my inspection point under the kitchen sink. At least there *was* a kitchen sink.

"Well, bye then!" called Bud.

"Yup!"

*****

Exactly two weeks later, Bud was back as promised. He had Harry in tow this time, plus a big box of supplies for me, including drills, chainsaws, other construction tools, and some ammunition. "Picked up a few more essentials for you," Bud said. "I saw you had ordered a bunch of things from the store in town."

Bud and Harry were both horrified to find that I had mostly been living off fish and carrots for the past two weeks. "Hunter-gatherer," I said, as I left them standing on the half-finished new porch and took the supplies into my shack. I unpacked quickly on my half-finished new bench, and saw that they had added some comfort food to the box. *Probably just as well they hadn't known about my pantry limitations, otherwise they might have bought me the whole damn grocery store.*

Bud and Harry never asked again if I was OK, but after they left that day, I did secretly enjoy the pizza and chips.

My shack was one big room. Laid out over 500 square feet, it was tiny in anyone's book, but to me, it really was paradise. Entry was off the front porch. Cupboards and a kitchen bench and sink were in the middle of the room. Fireplace, open cabinets around the walls, one comfortable chair. I made a footstool from discarded wood that I assumed Big Red had cut from fallen trees. My double bed. A folding table. An old tub for washing, an outhouse between the two shacks. No running water, no electricity. Perfect for me. My van had been my oasis, but once the roof was on the shack, I moved in. The first night in my new dwelling I slept very, very well. I agreed wholeheartedly with Big Red's hand-etched 'Paradise' sign, and had affixed it prominently above my new porch. I had hope that I was walking into my greatest season to an aligned life, as I felt more at home and more alive than I ever had before.

*****

Mother and Bess had visited me twice so far – once three weeks after I'd arrived, and again a month after that.

"Good Lord, Emmy-Lou!" Mother had expressed her concern on their first visit. "What have you gotten yourself into? So much work! This place is a wreck!"

Not sure what she had expected. Good thing she didn't see it when I first arrived...

Bess and Mother slept in the van that night, while I bunked in the back seat of their car. The next morning when we got up for 5.00 am coffee, they walked stiffly and held their backs and groaned, so I figured they didn't sleep too well.

"When I'm settled in to 'Paradise' I'll fix up that second shack and that can be your own cabin," I promised.

That made them both smile, as they sat cupping their coffee mugs like the coffee needed to warm them from the inside out.

On the following month's visit, they were very impressed.

"Wow, Emmy-Lou, so much progress!" Mother glowed.

Bess was happy for me, too. "You look so well rested. But don't you get lonely or bored with nothing to do out here?"

Nothing to do. Wow, really!

I suspected they wouldn't understand even if I tried to explain it.

*****

The banks of the river were a wild larder. I took my forage basket and collected a variety of nature's gifts. Sloe berries (I wanted to make gin), blueberries, crab apples, juniper berries, sorrel, dandelion, burdock, nettle, rosehip, mint, spruce tips, arnica, borage, elderflower, horseradish, and all manner of other greens. Food and medicine alike.

My cultivated garden was well re-established. I cleaned everything up and put my green thumb to good use. I had decided I was going to prepare and stay for winter, so I had a lot of work to do. Big Red must have been a bit of a survivalist, because I found many useful things of his, both in the remains of his cabins while I was restoring them, and while walking around the property.

I worked hard, and long, to be able to stay on my place year-round, no matter what harsh winter weather might come. I dug storage cellars and I filled them to the brim. I made a pontoon down on my slice of the river. I built a deck off my porch, and made a fire pit and grill place.

I loved being off the grid. I didn't even have a phone. I wasn't in anyone's reach anymore, not if I didn't want to be. I felt at one with nature and the frequency of the earth. I redeveloped my childhood imagination. Deer, guinea fowl and Canada geese would come and inspect me while I sat by the river and sang, and played at 'drums' with the rocks and sticks. The winter was long and I saw no other human for months, but I kept the same routine day in and day out, and I survived and I thrived. I slept well most nights. I felt like static energy started to gather all around me day after day; new sounds also developed around me like a hum as the spring blossomed and I did too.

My soul was all cleaned up.

*****

Bud and Harry had turned out to be more helpful than I originally had expected, and the townsfolk too seemed most dedicated to helping me. Perhaps I had now been here long enough to be considered a local. As spring turned into summer, trucks arrived with my new lumber orders, and all manner of other supplies were delivered regularly too. I started expanding my 'Paradise' cabin, and I was working on the second shack as well – now that it was warm again I was looking forward to receiving two or three visits from Mother and Bess over the next several weeks. First a new leak-proof roof for the second cabin; next some lean-to extensions and some 'plumbing' refinement for my own cabin (I now had an outhouse AND an 'inside bathroom'!). I was busier than ever and I loved it.

Late in July, Harry graded my driveway for me, as smooth as he could reasonably get it, and he invited himself to stay for the three days it took him to do it. He bunked down in his truck both nights, and we shared all our meals and talked about almost everything under the sun.

Once I was confident that my driveway now wouldn't bounce animals to death in the transport, I told Bud that the next thing on my list was livestock, specifically chickens. Bud informed me he had four orphans and he would be bringing them over the next day. (He really had meant it when he said, "At your service!") Early the next morning I heard a truck pull up and Bud's voice called out, "A dump and run job, sorry Em!" And then he was gone before I could blink twice, the sound of his truck fading quickly away.

New sounds on the porch made me throw open the front door and rush outside. Hoofbeats! And bleating! Not four chickens, but four snowy white GOATS!

I was delighted, but how did he know?

Ah, yes. Harry and I had shared a LOT of information about each other during his driveway-smoothing stay. I shook my head ruefully. Too talkative, yes, but I wasn't going to say no to the goats!

The said goats had disappeared around the back of my cabin. I went to rescue my vegetable garden.

*****

Harry was visiting again. He seemed nervous, and I caught a little of it. He said he had something for me.

For the first time in his presence I was slightly fearful, but I was intrigued as well.

He went to his truck and soon came back with a box. He made me turn away from him while he unpacked it on my kitchen bench.

"OK, you can turn around now."

Harry was standing by the bench, smiling. The bench now contained a bottle of champagne and a frosted cake with a '35' candle and a sparkler on top.

I had totally forgotten it was my birthday.

And I really *had* said too much to Harry.

"Happy birthday, Em!" said Harry. And then he popped the champagne and he lit the candle and the sparkler and then *he actually sang 'Happy Birthday' to me!*

Eventually I managed to choke out a thank you. I wasn't sure what Harry wanted from me. He was nice, yes, but not *that* nice. And besides, he was barely 22 years old.

We drank a toast to me, and ate some cake, and just talked, and laughed. I relaxed, and poured myself a second glass of champagne. Harry was just finishing his third.

He must have realized I had been nervous of him earlier. "It's OK, Em," he said. "I can't drive home, so I'll bunk in my truck tonight. But there's something I want to show you. Will you come and see, outside?"

The champagne hit me when I stood up, but I successfully made it outside. Sundown was just fading into full darkness. Harry grabbed my hand and made me run with him. "Hurry, I want to show you something!" he said again. "And I bet you haven't seen it before!"

I thought this was a silly thing for him to say – it was my place, and I'd been here nearly a year. *I've seen everything, man!* I felt myself giggling as I ran along, and Harry was giggling too. I wasn't sure if it was the sugar rush or the champagne or something else, but we were both running and giggling and it seemed natural, and for the first time since I was a teenager I felt happy, free, and blissful in the company of someone else.

"Come on!" Harry urged again, and we ran and panted and giggled, past pine trees, and down a little hill, to splash our feet across a shallow sandy creek bed.

The stars shone brilliantly bright as we ran up from the creek and out into a large flat open field.

"This is The Meadow," said Harry. "It was Big Red Dumfries's favorite place here. Have you been here at night and seen what happens?"

I was speechless. I hadn't been here *at all* – I didn't even know this place existed. *Why had I not found this place, and HOW had I not found this place?*

My expression said it all.

I squeezed Harry's hand. I felt a jolt of emotion course through my body, and my heart raced in a different way.

"Here, sit," said Harry, as he gestured to a flat structure on the grass. A little wooden dock, basically a raft. "I helped Dumfries drag this up from the river." This was the first time I recalled anyone indicating actually being friends with Big Red.

The sound of humming in many different tones surrounded us; varied frequencies. It felt like time stood still and that storms came and went. Harry kissed me. It felt so good but I knew it had to be so wrong. He was so very young. I found myself kissing him back.

"Em, you are so beautiful."

It was just the two of us, and all the frequency all around us. It felt natural, blissful, right.

With great effort, I pushed myself away from him. "We can't do this," I said. I changed the subject. "You knew him well, then, Big Red?"

Harry looked at me intensely, and then accepted the change. "Sure did," he replied. "Since I was in high school."

His eyes suddenly widened and became darting. He squeezed my hand again and got to his feet, pulling me with him. "Look, wait and watch, and shhh!"

My hair was very long now and it was all standing on end with the sudden increase of static electricity in the air. A lightning bolt crashed in front of us and I flew backwards. Harry was behind me and he caught me in his arms and hugged me tight. "It's OK, it's OK. Watch!"

It was like the northern lights had actually fallen out of the sky; aurora borealis on steroids. Bright green flashes, mesmerizing ribbons of purple, stunning scintillating whorls of iridescent pink and blue and yellow, all dazzling us for several minutes. Then it was gone in an instant.

My heart was pounding.

The starlight seemed to have faded now and it was very dark again. Harry grabbed a flashlight from his pocket and turned it on dull mode. "How was that? Best birthday present ever?" He was showing his age by the way he spoke.

"HARRY!" I said, stunned almost speechless. "What is this?"

"Em, actually I have no idea, but Dumfries and I would come here. He came here most every night, actually. Strange thing, you can't feel it or see it from the treeline or back further at all; you have to be here in The Meadow just after sundown. Weird, huh?"

Another great understatement.

We sat in The Meadow together for a long time.

*****

After that first time in The Meadow, I became *obsessed*.

Harry had stayed the night with me, on my birthday, after we had eventually returned from The Meadow. He didn't go to his truck, but stayed with me in my bed in the cabin. We just cuddled and kissed, again and again. And then I slept so well next to him, the best I had slept in longer than I could recall.

In the morning he stroked my wayward wet hair after I had showered. We drank coffee in silence and he looked at me with such admiration that I almost wished things could be different.

"I'm sorry, Harry," I said eventually, gently, and took his hand, "but we can't do this again. Thank you for my birthday; it was a new kind of magic I've never experienced before."

Harry had departed without another word, and I had immediately gone back to The Meadow, finding it easily now. In the daylight it looked like any conventionally gorgeous tree-lined field sprinkled with wildflowers, albeit wildflowers whose patterns were broken up by the incongruous presence of a small wooden dock. There was otherwise nothing out of the ordinary – no sign of anyone having recently walked over the grass, and no sign of a lightning strike.

From then on I went to The Meadow daily, both in the morning and back each night. Every night was different. The static was the same, coming and going, but the lights were always different. Such mixtures of color, brightness, rhythm, size, pattern and movement – familiar and repeating elements sometimes, but each night's overall display was as unique as if created by a celestial kaleidoscope.

For 100 straight days and nights I visited The Meadow and experienced the special aurora, and they were the best 100 days of my existence. It was so magical when the first light snows came. Not a single snowflake dropped on me as I sat in The Meadow – it was as if there was a protective layer of some kind above. Snow landed on the ground all over my property, except on The Meadow.

*****

Thanks to my Maisie-goat who had a fondness for the tough weeds around the base of my well, I discovered a concealed hidey-hole compartment that had been cleverly carved out of one of the well's exterior stones. Maisie-goat was keeping me company as I was drawing some water. I took notice when she stopped making weed-chewing noises and started making plastic-chewing noises. I took her new prize snack away from her immediately and discovered that it was a book, well sealed in plastic wrap and a plastic bag (now partially chewed).

That was on day 101, and that night I didn't go to The Meadow. Instead I sat in bed, wearing my battery operated headlamp, and opened the book. It had belonged to Alasdair Dumfries, and it was full of handwriting and sketches. I thumbed through it carefully, and page by page familiarized myself with Big Red. The book contained everything from the original construction plans of the two shacks, useful facts, gardening and farming plans (including a list of plant foraging locations), quotes, and a number of what appeared to be rough personal diary entries.

I noticed that the last entry in the book was July 19th, more than three years ago. I had eventually shown enough curiosity about Big Red's demise such that Bud had told me that someone from town had found his body in a field on August 26th of that same year...so, about five weeks after this diary entry. There was no apparent reason for his death, so Big Red was deemed to have died of a heart attack, in his mid-sixties. Nothing extraordinary about that. Bud said he'd had no known family. Bud and Harry had been practically the only people at his funeral.

The second winter on my place was proceeding much like the first, but now with occasional visits to The Meadow (surrounding snowfall permitting) and a lot of study of Big Red's book. I became as obsessed with the book as I was with The Meadow.

Dumfries was a town in Scotland, I knew, and in the book there was a list of dozens of Scottish Gaelic names. I wondered if the list actually represented Big Red's family. The book spanned years and years, several decades at least, although unfortunately a good deal of the earlier entries were illegible to me. Of the newer entries I was able to read, many were in point form, often of a fairly philosophical nature, and all quite intriguing to me.

One entry: *Question – Loneliness, or bliss? Answer – Perspective.*

Another: *Trust no one, not even your own eyes. Only trust the feelings you get.*

And yet another: *Strange becomes reality; accept what is near you and use it for enlightenment.*

I could see a progression of psyche; a development and an ascension from one way of thinking and being to another. Curiously I saw that the front of the book even looked like it contained different handwriting, and it harbored a faded name that I was finally able to just make out: Harrold Levi Ushkowitz.

*****

Mother and Bess came to visit early during the following spring, a few weeks after the last snow had thawed. Mother especially had suffered from the summer heat during their few visits last year, with no modern temperature control in their cabin, so I had told them to visit next in cooler weather. They had obeyed. To my surprise, they had brought Lilly with them this time. "She wants to live here, too," said Mother.
You mean YOU want her to live here...
But I was actually delighted. The goats were great, but they weren't indoor pets. Lilly settled down on my bed as if she had never slept anywhere else.

I had not seen Harry since that day after my last birthday. Bud started visiting again after the thaw, though. He told me that Harry had found himself a girlfriend, and was 'pussy whipped'.
Oh, Harry.
Bud also told me that Harry had been very depressed over much of the winter. "He was madly in love with someone, he finally told me, but it just didn't work out. Hit him very hard, apparently. First loves – you know how it is!"
I blushed. Thank God I had my back to Bud.
I controlled myself and changed the subject. "Bud, do you know who Harrold Levi Ushkowitz might have been?"
Bud froze. "Harrold Senior. My father, Em."

He breathed heavily and blinked rapidly, but I didn't notice at first. Bud and Harry shared the surname of Asher, and I was just about to ask about the discrepancy, when Bud pre-empted me. "Dad legally changed his surname to Asher just before he met Mom – said it was easier to get a job with a 'more boring' surname. But his father, my grandfather, was furious, so whenever it wasn't legally important Dad just kept using the Ushkowitz version. We named Harry after Dad, but Dad never knew his grandson. Dad just vanished one day back in 1996. I never talk about him. I didn't think Harry ever talked about him, either. Is that where you got the name?"

I sidestepped that question by asking one of my own: "Were Harrold and Dumfries friends, too?" I cleared my voice and was lucky that Bud was still too shocked to notice my residual embarrassment.

"Where are you getting all of this?" frowned Bud. "Harry is the only one who called Big Red 'Dumfries'. Sounds like you and Harry have been hanging out and getting closer than I thought. Em?" He looked sideways at me, and I felt my cheeks flush again. It had been a while since Bud had pointed his 'cop face' in my direction.

"No, Harry doesn't come here much these days, Bud – too busy with new friends, I guess," I tried to sound innocent and light-hearted as I spoke the truth.

Bud could have easily pushed more on my sudden knowledge of and interest in his father, but he didn't – I suspect he didn't really want to know. Instead he changed the subject, promising to get Harry to resume regular visits with me now that both his love-life and the weather were good again. I wondered if he would succeed.

*****

Lilly loved her new home, five hours' drive away from her old one. I loved having her with me. We did everything together, including foraging in all the places listed in Big Red's book. The river produced some amazing asparagus, the salmon came and went, and I filled all of my winter stores. Lilly especially loved the spoils of our fishing trips. I preserved fruit and bottled and canned as best I could. I made jam and even the best apple cider.

Bliss became me.

I still hadn't seen anything more of Harry, but Mother and Bess were coming back for their final 'acceptable weather' visit soon. I supposed I should head into town after I finished my morning coffee, to phone them and find out their plans.

I saw Bud driving slowly along the driveway. He parked and got out of the car, limping more than usual as he came to the porch. There was no shout out to me to put on fresh coffee. He just stood in the front doorway and stared inside. His face was a white as a ghost.

"Bud?" I jumped up in alarm. "Bud?"

"Em, there has been an accident out on the highway." All he could muster was a raspy whisper. "A multiple fatality. All four of them…" He didn't even blink.

"Bud?" I was so confused. My eyes widened. "Oh Bud, is it Harry? Oh no, no! Oh, Bud!" I choked out.

"Em…" Bud croaked, meeting my eyes for the first time, "it's all of them. It's Harry, his girlfriend, and Bess and your mother. A head-on collision last night…"

For a few seconds I was stunned. *They never do surprise visits…* Then I dropped to the floor, Lilly jumped up on top of me, Bud sat down next to me, and we cried and cried and cried together.

*****

That night, I needed to feel something. Something *else*. Lilly and I went to The Meadow. I sat on the little dock, on soft pillows, with Lilly tucked inside my shirt as usual. I felt stitched into the landscape as the static came and went, the humming rose and fell, the green aurora ribbons curled and glowed, a lightning strike cracked, and pink vortexes swirled. Then it was over. Lilly came out from under my shirt, and we just sat. This would be my new normal.

There was a rustling in the treeline to my right. For the first time, I took a small black canister of bear spray out of my pocket. I put it on the dock, next to my right leg. Lilly sat to attention, and began to purr intensely. She curled her tail around my arm.

"Hello?" I shouted, and waited. "Hello?" Nothing.

I scooped up Lilly and we retreated back to our cabin. We went to bed, but sleep never came that night. I had too many thoughts of Bess and Mother never enjoying a visit here again. Ever again. Ever again. Sadness filled each cell of my body. Memories crowded my mind.

Oh God, WHY?

In the morning, Lilly was just gone. So were my chickens and my goats. I searched everywhere I could think of. No sign of any of them, no signs of predation on them. Then I noticed there were no wild bird sounds either, and no rustling of a breeze in the trees. NOTHING?

"What's going on around here?" I called. I wasn't scared. I was calm, almost blank, all day. It was like I was the only person in the world.

As I walked to The Meadow that night, I felt as if my body was being stretched like spaghetti in a black hole. I looked at my forearm and hand – nothing unusual. I could hear and feel the static, and the frequencies of humming.

Now I could see black-cloaked figures around the edge of The Meadow, moving among the bordering trees. A boxy open structure reminiscent of a church was standing at the far end of The Meadow. Indescribable noises came from all directions. Honeycomb formations popped up all over The Meadow, along with the visage of a huge fluffy smoky face.

I looked to the little dock, and there sat Mother, Bess and Harry, with Lilly sitting beside them and curling her tail around Harry's arm. *WHAT?* Floating structures akin to glamping pods, hundreds of them, hovered or were suspended above us. The noise was green. There were multicolored auroras and green and purple vortexes.

"This is the history of the future, Em!" Harry shouted out to me, and beckoned to me to come to them. *WHAT IS HAPPENING?* There was more humming in different tones, different frequencies. Storms came and went overhead, above the invisible protective canopy.

"Once you have changed your mind, you can't go back to the way it all was before!" Mother called to me.

"I know I am someone's daughter!" It was Bess who shouted to me now. "It's this 'life' thing, Emmy – it never gives up its secrets! It's a Terra Experiment! It's a thought experience!"

I suddenly felt that I could relax. I let it all go, and had the sensation of my life being in perfect flow, somehow. I reached out to touch them all, these apparitions of my lost loved ones, and it was like they were really sitting there.

"But what *is* happening? I'm still so confused," I said to them.

They all started talking at once, explaining as best they could, up against my inadequate ability to understand very much at first. We continued to sit together – talking, listening, relaxing. Waiting.

*****

The sign was posted only in the realty building's window, at first.

The town thought they would like a local to buy, but realistically they knew that the locals might be a bit spooked. After all, it was the second time in four years that the property had been listed for sale as a deceased estate. This time, however, the cabins were fully renovated, the gardens were impeccable, and the fruit trees were producing a bumper crop every year. The well water was very sweet. It was still off-the-grid living, but it was extremely comfortable. The double residence at the end of the long and smooth and incredibly scenic driveway might even make for a good Airbnb investment.

The new realtor was confident that he had a winner and would eventually make a good sale.

The right buyer was certain to come along.

*****

I never 'fought' with the wild. I lived harmoniously with it. Now I just felt strange. I felt relaxed, but my heart was pounding. I was a little breathless, and my palms were sweaty too.

Other hologram people were now gathered around the large spruce trees, while those standing closer to me faded until they were gone. A swirling mass of air formed about 50 feet from my right side, like a mini tornado funnel, and then another.

The figure of a human, a woman, emerged from the nearest funnel and moved towards me. She was a mirror image of me. Another me.

Mother, Bess and Harry all smiled.

"Hi, Neiman," the mirror-woman said, smiling down at me too.

"Hello," I said hesitantly. "I'm Em. What's going on?"

I was still sitting on the little dock. The mirror-woman reached her hand down and offered me the object she held. It was a pearlesque sphere about the size of a golf ball. "You'll need this," she said, still holding out her hand, balancing the pearl ball on her cupped palm.

I reached out for it.

"Yes," said the mirror-woman me. "You're done with here now. You've completed it all."

I felt myself stand up. I felt so light. I felt like I was suddenly late for something. Yes, I was running late.

My previous residual depression lifted and I felt the fullness of all the love I held inside me. The other me touched my hand. She was icy cold. But somehow, so was I. Looking down at myself I saw that I too was now a hologram, a misty apparition even, and I was floating above the ground of The Meadow. I looked over to the little dock. Yes, I was still there, too. Or at least my previous body was, curled around in a fetal position on the dock. Now it was all becoming clearer; I knew what was going on.

Three more hologram copies of me came out of their little tornadoes and all beckoned to me to do something to the pearlesque ball that my new hologram form now held.

I had a feeling that everything that I had ever dreamed of had just come true.

Other Mother holograms appeared now, and other Besses, and other Harrys. All of us got up to leave, together. Because they were all done with here too.

"You'll get used to it again," the others all said in unison. "You've been here such a very long time."

Lilly whirled around me again as my pearl sphere lit up. My hologram fingertip had found a little ridge on the ball and traced it. An electrical blue light flashed over the ball and I was now inside a large transparent orb of my own, with Lilly by my side. I looked back at the little dock for the last time, and saw that my former body was gone.

The final tie was severed.

Everything seemed important all at once, and it simultaneously seemed like nothing was important ever. All I knew was that I was conquering my life, no – my EXISTENCE – in the way I FELT it was meant to be. I was no longer too much, I was MORE than enough.

It was time to move forward.

I reached down and patted Lilly's head. She felt fluffy and warm and she licked my fingers.

*****

"The analysis of your findings and testing is almost complete. So when you're ready, we will be very interested to meet with you to go over your results and discuss the details of your experience within the experiment. You did very well, Nita. Really – most excellent work. Congratulations. And welcome home."

10. Hot-Headed.

I grew up on Mount Stupid, but I wanted so much MORE; I wanted to move away and never come back. I felt I deserved more than the status quo and the sum of my childhood surroundings. As I grew older I avoided the mountain township and instead I frequented the beautiful beachside town of Hayes that was to be found at the end of a long drive out of York's Landing. Sometimes I pretended I lived there, instead.

Even though York's Landing (Stupidville!) held many fond memories for me (including young loves that were sweet but never quite realized…), it was still my dream to leave. And so, eventually, I did.

Sometimes it felt to me like the world wanted us (me!) to feel alone and disconnected. And I wanted to be the person who said, "I want to do this one thing!" and then actually do it.

So I did. I am that person.

I've even been portrayed as 'formidable' in the media. There, I am 'Pepper, the Formidable Olympic Walker' – that is exactly what they called me.

I guess that means I've done my worldly thing.

I had met a man, Alex Barnes, who had swept me off my feet. I could have never guessed where 'home' was for him…but yes, it was York's Landing. I didn't remember ever meeting him or even hearing about him when I was young and still living in York's Landing too. I guess I had spent more time in Hayes than I realized.

Alex and I got married, and we moved 'back to base' – yes, it was York's Landing, of course. Now that I was famous, my return 'home' was an occasion. The town gave us a ticker-tape parade down Main Street, and then we felt we were entitled to start our normal married life.

*****

Alex and I settled down; he found his feet quickly, while I took a more leisurely path of months to reacquaint myself with the place. I noticed more about the town now. Little had I known as a child that the very place I lived was a most extraordinary place with the most unusual people, always wanting and creating more. I had had zero idea about the reality of the town when I moved away by necessity, until I later moved back by choice.

More than the town itself, I spent a lot of my time in nature. I went daily to explore the mountains that seemed to spring up not too far from our back door – the exact area I had avoided in my childhood. I was seeing a lot of things with fresh eyes, and finding many of them amazing. The forest was so quiet and so beautiful. I could hear the water drip off a leaf. I could see and hear all the birds, and I never felt the air so fresh, especially once winter arrived properly and brought so much snow.

The snow made the going harder but I was determined to not let it stop me with my explorations. With that persistence, one day I made my way up a steep embankment, and over the other side was a large, dilapidated structure that took me by surprise. I examined it and saw that it was once a working timber mill. I did have a vague recollection of knowing such a business had existed, sometime in the York's Landing past.

Apparently, the grapevine had been talking; I didn't even know how it knew. But that evening my husband said to me, "You sneaker! You were up at the old timber mill, by yourself. What were you doing up there – don't you know that's too close to that unstable ridge?"

It was clear he wasn't happy with me. I didn't know what to say.

Alex continued, with a frown and just an edge of bitterness, "We can't leave it to Travin to check up on you all the time."

Well, I supposed that explained it, at least. My childhood friend, Travin, who was pretty much the only person I had cared to properly reconnect with when I had returned to York's Landing. Travin was checking on me still, like he always used to do years back. Still being my guardian angel. And Alex hated that, clearly.

"I was worried about you!" continued Alex. "I called three times and you didn't answer!"

No, I didn't answer, I thought. I had ignored my Scooby Doo theme ringtone – I was busy. Maybe I should have answered.

Alex hugged me so tight then, and every day of the following week. I thought he was being a bit dramatic. So I didn't tell him when I went back to the mill, and I hoped that the 'grapevine' wouldn't either. And I made sure that Scooby Doo didn't need to play for too long before I answered Alex's calls.

One evening Alex hugged me tight as usual, before I'd even gotten out of my layers of outdoor clothing, and exclaimed about me being bumpy. I emptied my coat pockets and showed him my collection of pinecones, remarking that they were probably the last of the season.

What I failed to tell him was that I had almost broken my leg, after falling from a weather-worn table I'd pulled under one of the mill windows and stood on in an attempt to get a proper look inside the mill. I was just trying to make out the items I could see, when the table toppled and only a fortunate snow pile prevented anything worse than a doozy bruise that I was sure would make itself known on my rump in a few short hours.

"Is your phone not ringing?" asked Alex. "I've been calling you – are you not answering? Or perhaps you can't hear Scooby Doo under all that wool you're wearing?" He chuckled to himself and added, "And I can't believe you paid money for that ringtone – they are free now, you know, silly woman!"

He laughed and pulled me into his chest and kissed me wildly.

I had two thoughts almost simultaneously.

Oh no, my phone is missing!

I think Alex is jealous of Travin.

I did recall on a couple of occasions Travin saying that he didn't trust my husband, citing, "Alex has bad blood in his lineage."

My main problem was more immediate though than Alex's blood – his wrath if I had to confess that I had lost my phone, most likely in the snow underneath the window of the mill.

Fortunately Alex seemed to have other things on his mind.

"Are you going to make those Texas Roadhouse rolls for me tonight?" Alex whispered, as he nibbled on my ear. "Sparky shot some squirrels today, up over the ridge. I'll cook them up with a bit of cream, garlic, salt, pepper, and mushroom – yum?"

"And rosemary?" I asked, as I also nodded about the rolls.

"Oh yes, I'll go get some fresh sprigs off Mom," he smiled. "See how convenient it is, living here now?"

*****

"*Scooby Dooby Doo where are you we got some work to do now!*" rang out musically from just beneath the snow.

And stopped.

And began again.

The mill's side door next to the window was partially obstructed by the little table that had been toppled over earlier in the day. The door opened a crack. A large hairy hand sporting excessively dirty yellow fingernails reached out through the slim gap, pushed the table a little to get it out of the way, and fished out the phone from its frosty hiding place.

Leaving my dough to rise, I thought I would just have time to go fetch my phone while Alex was busy with squirrels and cast iron cookware, and was under the impression I was taking a nap anyway. The pre-dusk temperature had dropped and I was rugged up so roundly I could have been mistaken for Humpty Dumpty (I was finished with great falls, though, I hoped!).

I made it up to the mill promptly, to where the little table lay. I could not see my phone. I searched ever more frantically as time ticked away – soon the squirrels would be done and my cover would be blown.

"*Scooby Dooby Doo where are you we got some work to do now!*" suddenly sang out, faintly, from inside the mill. I stood as tall as possible and looked through the window as best I could. Nothing.

The ringtone sounded again and again, and got louder as I followed it around the side of the mill, and went down some steps to a lower level which was clear (had been cleared?) of snow. Looking through an apparent basement window at ground level, I could see into a sunken room. My phone was on a large table in the middle of the room. It was no longer ringing.

"Hello!" I knocked wildly on the windowpane, "that's my phone in there and I need it back, please!"

Nothing.

"HELLO!" I shouted again. Still no response. Shit, I didn't have time for this! The wind was picking up and snow was starting to drift in. There was a door on this side of the mill, too, but like every door I had already tried, it was locked. Shit, shit. It was getting dark.

"*Scooby Dooby Doo where are you we got some work to do now!*" came the tease of my phone once more.

"HELLO HELLO HELLO!" I screamed. "HELLO, I NEED TO GET MY PHONE!"

It was as futile as ever. I abandoned the retrieval attempt, descended the mountain with almost dangerous haste (I had slipped over before!), and arrived home just in time not to be missed.

"These are so good, babe," said Alex, half an hour later, as he ripped up the fresh buttery Texas Roadhouse rolls and mopped up the pan juices and sauce from the squirrel meal.

*****

The overnight snowfall had been particularly thick. The middle-aged couple sat in their chairs on the porch admiring it and how beautiful it looked on the maple trees. They drank their coffee just as they did each morning at this time just after sunrise. They dunked maple-sweet buns into their steaming mugs – a 30-year tradition.

A familiar man, fully covered in bulky cold-weather gear and holding a shotgun casually at his side, came picking his way carefully through the snow on the driveway and towards the porch.

"Mornin'!" called out the man on the porch. "Have we got bears?"

The bulky man gestured back to the line of woods.

The couple on the porch suddenly felt very unwell. The husband vomited. The wife got to her feet, gasped, then clutched her throat and fell forward, motionless, onto the wooden planks of the porch. The husband stayed seated but reached his hand out towards the bulky man, not saying a word, but pleading with his eyes for help.

The bulky man raised his shotgun and fired into the husband's chest.

The bulky man listened, but heard nothing after the echo of his gun. He then walked right to the edge of the porch, aimed for the back of the wife's head, and fired again. "Just to make sure," he whispered.

The bulky man left via the footprints he had already made. Not that it would matter soon – the new snow falling fast and thick would fully cover his tracks.

*****

I'd had only one thought when I woke: *I have to get my phone!*

"What are your plans today, babe?" I asked Alex, over our morning coffee. It was just before dawn, pitch dark, and absolutely freezing. I stoked the fire.

"I'm off to see Mom and Dad just after sunrise, grab some maple buns," he replied. "Then I'll head to Main Street to SUZI'S to see Lyndsey. She wants some information from me for an article. I'll grab some cactus juice shots too, while I'm there – that will warm us up."

His words were bland but his tone seemed stern. He was grumpy, or focused – I couldn't figure which.

He gave me a peck on the cheek. "Stay safe," he said, as he went out the door. He took his Remington with him, but surreptitiously. He probably thought I didn't see him leave with it.

I waited an hour or so, until the new snowfall had stopped and it was fully light. I dressed as Humpty Dumpty again and made my way back to the mill.

As I approached the mill I thought I heard a noise behind me, and I looked back. No one was there, but my heart was pounding. I breathed in and out deeply, and the frosty air calmed me.

I headed around to where I had banged on the basement window the night before. I saw tracks in the new snow, that I knew had only finished falling a half-hour before. *So much for this place being abandoned,* I said to myself, thinking that perhaps whoever had been here last night was not just passing through after all.

I heard my Scooby Doo ringtone go off again, and I was just about to lean down to rap on the window when a loud gunshot came from inside the sunken room. I dropped to the ground and covered my head. Another shot followed almost immediately, then there were no sounds other than my phone ringing once more. My heart was pounding again and it was all I could do to raise my face far enough out of the snow to breathe.

Raising my head brought my eyes level with the basement window, and I could see perfectly into the sunken room. Four huge men stood in a loose circle by the table. They were hillbilly-looking and all had pure white hair, even though none of them appeared to be older than forty.

I gasped when I realized that there was a fifth person in the group, lying crumpled on a tarpaulin spread on the floor in the middle of the hillbilly circle. It was Alex. It was my husband.

I was too petrified to scream or move and could only watch as one of the hillbillies raised the gun he was holding and shot it for a third time, into the back of my husband's head. Another hillbilly was bending down to grab the handle of a trapdoor in the floor, and when the trapdoor was open, the murderer hillbilly and another one quickly rolled my husband's body up in the tarpaulin, and then kicked the whole arrangement into the open hole. They closed the trapdoor, moved the table over the top, and then the four of them walked out of my sight to somewhere else in the mill. All was eerily, deathly, quiet.

I felt that I could probably scream now but I had sense enough to know not to. I pursed my lips tightly closed. *Pull yourself together!*

I heard motors start up on the far side of the mill – snowmobiles, perhaps – then listened as the sound moved away into the distance.

Adrenaline surged through me. I was frightened, but I was also so so ANGRY. Without even thinking about what I was doing, I found myself kicking in all the glass of the basement window and throwing off my outermost coat in order to be able to squeeze through the opening I had made.

I tried to move the table away from over the trapdoor, but it was far too heavy for me. "Alex," I sobbed, trembling. There wasn't even any blood; no evidence of what had just occurred here.

I thought I heard the snowmobiles returning. *Shit!* I grabbed my phone off the table, switched it to silent, and squeezed back out of the window. I picked up my coat and started to run down the hill. I made for a rocky outcrop to hide behind, forgetting to be careful and that this was a path I had slipped on several times over the past few months. And so it was again, and I started to fall – a maneuver so familiar it almost seemed rehearsed.

Only this time, a set of strong arms caught me before I could slide down the hill.

"Fuck, Travin!" I squealed.

"Shhh, Pepper, SHHH!" Travin whispered desperately. "I've got you, shush, shush!" Quickly he covered my mouth with one snow-gloved hand and pulled me close against him under the overhang of the rock formation with his other. We were both silent and still, and the next moment we heard men speaking above us.

"Look," said a deep voice, "fresh footprints."

A second voice replied, "They are tiny prints. It's nothing, probably those damn vandal kids again."

The voices trailed away.

Travin held my mouth shut still. We sat motionless and silent for what felt like hours. Finally he took his hand away from my mouth.

"They killed Alex!" I released not only my breath but a cry.

"I know, I saw it all," Travin said, still holding me close. "I'm so sorry, Pepper. But Alex…Alex was a bad seed."

*****

Months later, after the sensation of Lyndsey's York's Landing Tribune article about Alex had died down, I had fully accepted that Travin and I were together, where we belonged.

Where I belonged, and where I had always belonged.

That day on the mountain, Travin had taken charge. "Say nothing about this if you want to live," he had stressed to me. "I've got you – I'll take care of everything. It's just York Justice."

He had taken me back to my house, looked after me, got the story straight, and had called the police. I had gone numb, and I let him do everything, whatever he thought was best.

Lyndsey's article was well researched and balanced as always, even with the references to grief and death and new beginnings and guardian angels that were turning into something of a signature of her writing these days. As for Alex's disappearance itself, there was nothing concrete known about that, only speculation. The townsfolk weren't short of opinions and they rehashed the checkered Barnes family history as much as they discussed the present scandal. York's Landing was pretty equally divided in concluding either that Alex had murdered his parents and then gone to live a secret life elsewhere, or that he had been a victim of some foul play too. I could – *I must* – ignore this chatter. I was formidable, and so I built a formidable wall around myself.

The mystery would probably never be solved.

The first time I had confessed to Travin that I loved him came soon after I acknowledged that I owed him my life.

I would never stop being grateful.

Travin and I lived together now, at his house, which felt like a home to me in a way every place before it had not; a way I had not even realized I had had before and then lost when I had first left York's Landing. It was funny to think now about what was less that I had had to lose, before I could find more.

Every night, Travin and I would sit on the couch, hand in hand, as we had done back when we were teens.

"I never stopped loving you," Travin would say, almost every night. And occasionally, he would add: "I am sorry about Alex Barnes. You weren't to know. But he was just too hot-headed for York's Landing."

❂❂❂

YOUNG: Collection of 2-Minute Tales.

THE SECRET OF BEING YOUNG

I remembered who I was as I looked outside at the rain. A simple drop among others.

Puddles are forming on my front porch, and the game has changed. It's hard work being someone you are not. It's exhausting, it's monotonous, it's a set of lies in motion that keeps thundering along and no doubt will end badly, but the unstoppable nature of it is addictive.

The act, the stress, and the lies – they all stopped this day…and now I'm the youngest I've looked and felt in 15 years.

I filled out a form. It was medically based and asked: 'Do you have prematurely ageing skin?' I ticked 'Yes', and in my mind it was a *HELL YES,* but I wanted to be a vessel of youth like my mother and sister.

I always swoop in with scrumptious things I've baked, and gifts from my heart, whenever others need assistance and reassurance. Others are there for me, too; but how I present is not what I really am.

I watched a video clip where several pink flamingos were wading and nibbling in the water. A fluffy white baby flamingo was there too and doing the same – twitching with energy, and gusto, and wonder. Each little feet 'tippy-tappy' it performed was delightful to watch, along with its little fluffy butt-wiggling. I'm 45 and this was the first time I had seen a baby flamingo!

What else haven't I seen, what else haven't I been doing, what MORE can I experience to receive the energy of wonder and embrace the envy of 'being young'?

I want to be adorable, loving, live a wondrous life…and tippy-tappy my feet in my front porch puddles.

***

"Promise me you'll always remember: You're braver than you believe, and stronger than you seem, and smarter than you think."
– A. A. Milne.

***

TODAY I PLAN TO BE MORE USEFUL THAN THE 'G' IN 'LASAGNE'

Useless. That is what I've told myself for eternity.

I've taught my shopping trolley not to veer into the Baskin-Robbins store when I complete a grocery run. We all know each one of those shopping carts has a mind of its own, but the ones I choose seem to be particularly disobedient.

So I ordered my groceries to be delivered. How was I to know that a stray box of Maxibon would be included in my order? I have to say I couldn't now deny myself a frozen treat.

I really didn't mind them, actually.

And I just opened the second box that somehow magically appeared in the freezer.

Don't struggle for 'perfection'. Perfection means finished, and we are never finished. This is a journey of the beautiful evolution of our soul.

CAPTAIN'S LOG, SUPPLEMENTAL

I've been told I'm little. Cute. I have been treated like a child my whole life. But maybe now I am actually 'old', with no bottom teeth, and I have a limp, too.

I have recorded a 'Captain's Log' style of diary all my life. I've been going back through it as I've been told I have only weeks to live. Revisiting the golden times. Trying to make my little life count. I thought I had more time.

Once you're done, there is no going back.

Revisiting my 'Captain's Log' has been amazing. I enjoyed my life all over again. I felt complete.

I just got off the phone with the hospital. There had been a terrible mistake. My diagnosis is incorrect – actually, they had the entire wrong person.

My health is all okay. I guess my 'reboot' leaves me to explore MORE of a life that I thought I never would get.

So I'll start my 'Captain's Log, Supplemental' now, and enjoy myself even MORE.

HAPPINESS IS WAITING (CHEESECAKE RECIPE)

I'm in the middle of making a no-bake chocolate fingers cheesecake. The chocolate fingers are a throwback, today, as I'm off to the UK on an adventure!

Happiness is waiting for me there.

This cake has a nice buttery digestive biscuit base (our USA friends can use Graham crackers), with a creamy chocolate cheesecake filling, and a smooth milk chocolate ganache topping. All of this is surrounded by chocolate finger biscuits as the showpiece. True happiness!

All you need is...

Biscuit base:

300 g digestive biscuits (or Graham crackers), crushed

160 g unsalted butter, melted

51 chocolate finger biscuits (approximately, depending on cake size – this number will be about right if you use an 8-inch springform pan but if you use a 9-inch springform pan instead then you will likely need additional chocolate finger biscuits to fit)

- Line the tin edge with upright chocolate finger biscuits.
- Mix the crushed biscuits and the melted butter and then press the mixture into the bottom of the cake tin.

Cheesecake filling:

350 ml double cream, cold

500 g cream cheese

120 g icing sugar (powdered sugar)

250 g milk chocolate, melted and cooled slightly

- Whip all the ingredients together and spread the mixture over the biscuit base.
- Refrigerate at least 4 hours or overnight to set.

Ganache topping:

100 ml double cream, hot (microwave for 1 minute)

200 g milk chocolate (bar or chocolate chips)

- Melt the chocolate into the cream and mix well.
- Cool the ganache a little, then pour it over the set cheesecake.

My tip – do life YOUR WAY. Eat the cake. Enjoy each bite. Travel, but before you go, make your favourite things. Happiness is in your hands.

***

"Play with willingness." – Marie Elson.

***

I AM DIFFERENT, NOT LESS

Mouse Castle.

To be at one with these glorious surroundings, and the dresser that lives here. We farm with Anglo-Nubian Roshane goats – we eat the cheese and yoghurt.

We witness the milking of the goats.

"Hi, guys," I say, in my best shepherdess voice. I was a natural. We stay and chat. They stare.

"Oh come on, darling – what could possibly go wrong?"

We are the mice of Mouse Castle.

We are different, not less than other residents.

***

"When things change inside you, things change around you."
– Anonymous.

***

THEY HAVE ESCAPED!

If you have light, or are finding your light, you just might have heard of this old cautionary adage: "Your light is going to irritate a lot of unhealed people."

Nevertheless, embrace your light. Don't be a disservice to yourself!

If you try to dim yourself, you no longer hold the space for yourself, or for others either.

What has you shining away? Has your fun escaped you? Has your laugh escaped you? Has your wit been hidden? All these shrink you. Have you not been, had you not seen, had your passion waned, had your sorrow pained?

A mystery of your light may bind you, may blind you, or even remind you; an escape from the freedom of yourself.

IS your happiness an elective?

Question: Loneliness, or bliss?

Answer: Perspective!

***

"Love all, trust a few, do wrong to none." – William Shakespeare.

***

KINKED: LIKE A HOSE HOLDING THE WATER BACK

I watch the water sprinkling through the nozzle of the hose. It seems so effortless, that the water just flows out. I kink the hose by folding it over on itself, and the water stops.

I've kinked my own life, and the flow has stopped.

I stare into the spray that has returned now I've let go of the restriction. The spray gives off prismed light – rainbows. I think of my friends all in the flow, and doubling down, and making a go of all that they do. I know life isn't a competition, but I'd be the wooden-spooner if it were. What would it look like for me to double down?

I hate what I do. I need to find something I like doing, like watering this

162

garden for my next-door neighbour. How can a wooden-spooner make a comeback? Later I will watch something, and it will inspire me until I think of my situation, and then I'll become depressed again. I'm tender, I'm soft, and I'm fragile.

"You've got no gumption!" my grandmother used to tell me. "You're always holding back!"

I look in the mirror, and all I see is restriction. Is that possible? What does restriction look like? My hair has a kink, my face has a kink, I see pressure building up in my eyes, I see a flushed face. I'm just a hose all wound around in a knot, with no hose reel to keep me in order. My life is kinked. I am my own boundary, my own limitation. I'm a lack of gumption and visibility. My interactions are tightly self-controlled. I finally admit it – I'm not free at all.

My friend mentions that they need a life model for her art class. She's shocked when I say I will do it. It's a watercolour class. How appropriate. Maybe it's a great way to unkink myself and let MYSELF flow.

I arrive at the class, and much to my horror I discover that being a life model means being naked. Gulp! But unkink, right? Right! So now I'm nude, sitting in a fake garden, holding a hose, with my own 'hose' dangling free. And yes, I'm blushing, but I hold my nerve, and I remain still, listening to the chit-chat around me.

"Your friend is so good!" one artist says to my friend. "He is a natural. Are you sure he's not a model?"

"He is now!" smiles my friend. "And he's a double natural, because he is also a gardener!"

"Really?" asks another student. "He can come and do my garden! Has he always been a gardener?"

"Actually his usual work is as an accountant," replies my friend, "but unhappily. He says he needs to unkink his life."

"Wow, no kinks there, he is a legend!" The conversation continues. "I want him to do my garden, too." "So do I!" "Me four!"

And so I make a simple decision of gumption, which allows me to find that visibility and free interactions can change everything.

These days I am a happy gardener and a professional art model – I'm unkinked, unrestricted…and booked out eight weeks in advance!

And the line I hear regularly now? "There's just no holding you back, is there?"

***

"We are tender and fierce. We are soft and strong. We are fragile and courageous. Sometimes all in one day." – Anonymous.

***

SOON I WAS MILKING FIVE GOATS TWICE A DAY

Eremition (noun): The act of gradually fading from the lives of others, not out of malice but out of a desire for solitude, renewal or reflection.

Over and over, I replay a video from Instagram.

A cute little blonde girl, maybe three years old, is standing at the window inside her lounge room. Looking at the camera, she points to the window and says to her mother (who is apparently the one filming), "A fucking goat outside!" Her mother responds, "It's just a goat!" But the little girl is not having that, as she frowns, points and looks outside again, and insists, "No! It's a fucking goat!" The mother then giggles and pans the camera to show the view through the window, to a suburban backyard, where there is in fact a small brown and white goat, eating the fallen leaves.

The video only goes for nine seconds, but it's hilarious, and deserves the multiple replays. I laugh until my face hurts and my sides do too, every time I either think about it, or watch it on replay.

I can relate!

As I look outside through the door of my hunting cabin, my shack, past the porch, I can see my own six fucking goats eating plants they shouldn't be. There is a vastness of vegetation on my 40-hectare property, and it's the goats' job to be consuming and clearing the grass and the blackberries and the other overgrown green debris.

But no, they eat my vegetable garden! The five female kids bleat and buck around, while an older billy who leads the herd is only slightly more sedate, but they all work together diligently to wreak havoc on the forbidden plants!

I can't help but chuckle, and as the kids mature I find myself gratefully having become a hermit – going from what others might call 'a normal life' to solitarily milking five nannies twice a day.

And giggling every time: "Fucking goats!"

***

"We delight in the beauty of the butterfly, but rarely admit the changes it has gone through to achieve that beauty."
– Maya Angelou.

***

BODY POSITIVITY

I wrote an article entitled: **Chasing Skinny, Chasing Strong**

My name is Lyndsey Lake. I run a cute little health food store on Main Street. I also do freelance journalism, which pays better than I expected, but maybe they're just very generous at the local newspaper, the York's Landing Tribune, where they publish my special articles.

The title of my article is a common saying in the gym community. But my intention was to affirm a body-positive image. This simply involves loving your body – regardless of size, shape, color or ability. Love your body, even if it's not skinny. Love your body, even if it's not strong. But if you do want to chase skinny or strong or something else? That's OK too! Body positivity is loving your body at all its stages, and along any journey between stages. What's in your skin is uniquely and iconically you, and that's always a cause for celebration and love.

My little store building is as iconic as the skin I reside in. Every day I run into interesting individuals and tell my guests about all the happenings in the town, and in my life. I tell each person that they have the right and opportunity to succeed and to love their day-to-day stories.

I must admit that I'm a little scared to plan and save – what if I wanted to do more? What if I got carried away with my dreams and goals? Do I have an endless bucket list? For many people, the legacy of my store and my writing would be enough for a bucket list. But maybe I want more.

If money were no object, I would leave America, and go to live on some remote Scottish island. Each morning I'd walk to the summit as my daily exercise. I'd congratulate myself, "Yay, you made it!" and on top of the hill would be the only place I could get good cell service. I'd take my carbon footprint very seriously. Solar power, gardening, a self-sustaining lifestyle. No electric bill, no car. I would read, and enjoy nature, and create art…

For now though, I live day by day, without expectations and with zero disappointments. That's something, and for some it's a sign they have really made it!

I no longer chase skinny, but I do chase strong and capable, and positive, no matter what that looks like. I live for positivity. I also live for my friend Suzi, now that she is no longer here. But in a way, I feel that she lives through me. She's part of my journey, and I embrace the journey, and love it with positivity. And I let myself be beautiful, for her, and for me, and for everyone around me.

***

"It is hard to be brave, when you're only a Very Small Animal."
– A. A. Milne.

***

THE APPLE BASKET

I'm not just me. I'm not perfect; in fact I'm a little tattered these days. I've held lots of importance during my many years. I've assisted with multiple generations of the same family, and I've witnessed many of their conversations. I've even featured unknowingly to others in many family portraits, selfies and TikTok clips.

"Ignore them."

"Just give it time."

"Don't compare."

"Stay calm."

"It's all on you."

"Wear a smile more often."

"Be yourself."

These are probably some of the best that I can recall.

I am an apple basket, living in a multi-level kitchen. I've been sitting here for 45 years, filling and emptying. My family has had so many kitchen moments! I have witnessed renovations and have been moved back and forth from one bench to another. I have spent some time in the kitchen hutch, and for one spring I sat on the kitchen windowsill, where I became sunbleached.

'Old Peggy' is my name. In earlier years there was an Aunt Peggy who lived in a sea cottage and enjoyed watching ships through her kitchen window. She loved basket-weaving and she made me, over many weeks, until her hands bled. She set me in my pride of place on the main kitchen bench, and filled me with fresh apples off her trees. I had cradled crab apples, bellflowers and pippins – all cooking apples, but beloved of scholarly types; Aunt Peggy had held her head high. I was handed down in the family, but unbeknownst to anyone I had a hidden secret.

"You know how you let yourself think that everything will be all right if you can only get to a certain place or do a certain thing?" This is the latest from my current family as they chat around me.

I have something else to consider. Perhaps we all have to meet our match sometime or other... A new basket has moved in. I'm at one end of the main bench and it's at the other. And we watch each other day in and day out.

"Don't move Old Peggy too far," the current mother says.

I'm a well-woven wood-bushel apple-orchard gathering-basket! I have been bleached and scratched over the years, I've moulded, I've been spray painted in spite, and I've even been shelved as just decor. But I'm now back in high vogue and I'm used and celebrated as an 'antique' and as an 'heirloom'.

"Oh, ain't that just DARLING?" grandmother-in-law said, the first time she saw me.

But no one has yet seen my hidden secret: *'Life is not a problem to be solved, but a reality to be experienced – S Kierkegaard.'*

This is boldly handwritten on a scrap of paper from Aunt Peggy's old recipe book. The parchment is neatly folded and rolled ever so tightly, and wedged snugly between my wooden slats and my well-worn willow weave. One day, perhaps, to be found.

Until then, I sit and watch my adversary at the other end of the kitchen bench.

***

All that we see or seem is but a dream within a dream.
– Edgar Allan Poe.

***

FILMING A MUSIC VIDEO

My extroverted self made some plans a couple of weeks earlier, but now my introverted self didn't want to friggin' go!

Out of nowhere there had been an inbound comment from a friend: "Hey, what are you guys doing on Friday in two weeks?"

"Why, not much really, how can we help?"

"I'm shooting a clip for my new single and need extras. It's a bar setting, and I'm needing customers to sit around type of thing."

"Sure, super fun!"

Bucket list item: Music video.

Reality: Freakin' freaky!

The enormity of the event hit me. BUCKET LIST ITEM – BE IN A MUSIC VIDEO.

The day arrived. It was almost snowing, and we drove hours north. There were film crews and scripts, but the lead actress was a no-show. It really was a Hollywood-style event.

We were upgraded from bar stool extras to actors and dancers with an actual script to follow. Definitely bucket list time!

My heart raced, my palms were sweaty, and then…we ACTED. We were in a bar brawl, we witnessed a murder, we ran, we barely escaped with our lives, we danced, we were homies and we were rappers.

Bucket list away…TICK!

Our work was released and sent out into the ether to be famous.

The day we filmed a music video…TICK!

This day was of immense personal significance. It was not just a favour for a friend, but the sense of accomplishment changed my persona.

I feel like I see facets of life differently now.

ARIES WORLD by **WILDCARD**
https://www.youtube.com/watch?v=sNSqOZ6kxsQ

***

"You can't use up creativity. The more you use, the more you have."
– Maya Angelou.

***

THE FORTUNE COOKIE

WHEREVER YOU GO, ELEVATE. So read the shred of paper from the sweet dessert treat.

The restaurant always served a bowl of fortune cookies as the finale to a meal, and Mother would always push the bowl away.

However, Father would open a few until he read the desired outcome. "See, Sandy, things WILL be all right!" he would spruik to Mother's scowling face. "Why won't you embrace change, Sandy? It's the plan to growth!"

The monthly family meal outing would then always end in the same way, with a silent ride home.

And so it was again today.

Back home, alone in my room, I pondered my own cookie's fortune once more: *WHEREVER YOU GO, ELEVATE.*

I got the same feeling from this instruction now as when I first watched the 1986 fantasy movie 'The Boy Who Could Fly'. I could relate. An unfortunate upbringing, an internally disturbed child, and an obsession with birds. I was like Eric in the movie, often standing on rooftops and window ledges posing with flying arms and imagining actually taking flight.

The thought electrifies me and sparks flight-of-fancy in my mind. That movie intrigued me; I still watch it often, even as an adult.

And I still feel the feeling of flight...

***

"Don't ask permission to fly. The wings are yours. And the sky belongs to no one." – Anonymous.

***

RAINY DAYS AND SUNSHINE

Why save for a rainy day when the sun is always shining?

My water bottle went on an adventure, and I couldn't have cared less for ANYTHING else in the world.

Today I did the impossible – I rediscovered the natural environment. I had read an article that advised that forest hiking was a fantastic activity for both the brain and body. I had always put off going to 'the outdoors'. I'm too tired after long workdays, I do house chores on the weekends, gym of course has to be done, and oh, always the groceries. I never had time for any of the 'fun stuff' – even my to-be-read book pile was put off for a rainy day.

But today I needed to improve my mood. I had heard the neighbours talk about a young family having moved in down the road – they had purchased the four hectares of land beyond the end of our street and had made it into a photographer's sanctuary. The bird boxes encouraged a great variety of birdlife to the area now, along with other bush creatures. The word on the street was that it was amazing, like a natural zoo or a wildlife refuge.

I was assuming physical activity at the end of my working day would make me more tired, but nevertheless I embarked on my pre-sundown stroll through the sanctuary. I felt the hormones that harboured my stress decreasing with each step. The forest initially seemed quiet, but I found myself listening first to my breath, and then to the sounds of the woods that were there after all, once I relaxed and became attuned to them. I could feel my worries extinguish. I felt like I could hear my blood flowing. I detected rustling in the trees, I felt the gentle breeze, and I listened to the chirping accompanying the evening roosting of contented feathered friends. I could duck into the blind hides here and there to witness the lives of the birds and other animals up close, without them having to be afraid of me.

It was truly a gift of animals and plants in their natural environment. The neighbours weren't one hundred per cent truthful. This was more than just a sanctuary – this was totally a magical getaway, where the pathway to the forest was like a bridge to paradise.

After walking the circuit twice, I stopped and stood with my arms outstretched and my face turned up to the waning sunlight, like I was about to fly. Why had I lamented and put this off for so long? And why am I saving my to-be-read pile of books for a rainy day when my life is shining now?

"'Just living is not enough,' said the butterfly, 'one must have sunshine, freedom, and a little flower.'"
– Hans Christian Andersen.

***

INTRUDER ALERT

I live by myself, but lately I'd had the feeling that I was no longer alone in my home. I've read about cases where people had squatters hiding and living in their attics or basements; strangers they never knew were there, not until something freaky happened, like a glimpse of something weird on a security camera.

I don't have an attic but I do have an unfinished basement. No security cameras, though. Last week I did a thorough check of the basement, even moving some stuff up into the bedrooms out of the way. I didn't see anyone down there. Not then, anyway.

I have no idea where this man came from – I just knew it was another man – but I certainly didn't let him in. I checked all my doors and windows; all locked. So he's clever, and very good at hiding. I know he's been eating my food, though. There's definitely stuff missing from my fridge, including my favourite ice-cream.

I don't have much faith in the police, at least not the new officers who came after Bill retired. Bill and I had gone to school together; I knew he was a good guy and a good cop. But because I didn't personally know anyone down at the police station now, I called my son instead and he came over to check my place out. It was his childhood home so he knew all the nooks and crannies. He did complain about all the extra stuff cluttering the bedrooms now, but I explained how I'd had to clear out the basement to check it.

My son didn't find the intruder either. I wasn't very surprised about this – he was always the worst of the kids at both hiding and seeking.

After my son left to return to his family I went into the kitchen to find something for dinner. That's when I noticed more problems in my fridge. I don't think anything else was *missing*, but it looked like some stuff had been *messed with*. What a loaded concept – *messed with*. Was that his game? He wasn't content to just 'share' my home...maybe he was planning to become the sole occupant?

That night I ate canned soup for dinner – a can that I opened brand new, and I didn't let the contents out of my sight while I ate.

Things have only gotten worse since then. I see more and more signs he's here, and getting bolder – things are moved around, including that he's taken some of the bedroom stuff back downstairs (possibly that's more cover to allow him to hide from me better). He's been taking my clothes, and leaving his dirty socks – that used to be my clean socks – on the floor in the basement. He's been opening my mail. Almost the worst of it is that he keeps doing the crosswords in my big puzzle book, and half the time he doesn't even get the answers right!

Sometimes I'm sure I see him ducking around a corner as I come out of a room; sometimes I get a glimpse of him in the hallway mirror, when he passes silently behind me. He's older than I thought he'd be, but clearly still pretty fit. I'm actually impressed at how he manages to avoid me. I'm sure now that he's poisoning my tea, and my instant coffee, and maybe even my jam. The jam smelled funny the other day, so I threw it out without eating any more of it. He won't get me that easily.

My son had asked me to come and stay at his home for a little while, to get a change of scenery and to enjoy a nice visit with my two young granddaughters. He didn't know the intruder was still in my home and getting bolder, and I didn't want to tell him; he's got his own concerns. I agreed to stay with them that night. My son came to fetch me and for once didn't criticise the untidiness of the house. I suppose the kitchen looked a lot neater since I had thrown away all the food the intruder could possibly have tampered with.

The next morning, my son and daughter-in-law left for work, taking their girls with them to drop off at school on the way. I went back to my own house – I had to know what the intruder had been up to. I discovered that he had been driving my car – it was now parked on the street (and not very neatly), instead of in the garage where I had last left it!

I was furious. I was even more furious when I realised that the front door was unlocked; I was able to just walk right in! And there, in the kitchen, were some grocery bags, half emptied. I checked the fridge and the cupboards, and sure enough, there were now replacements there for most of the things I had thrown out the other day. The intruder was restocking the kitchen, no doubt hoping I'd get bored or careless with my canned soup, and instead sample something to which he could easily have added any manner of sinister extras. There was even a new tub of my favourite ice-cream in the freezer. Some of it was already eaten – I guess he really does like that flavour too.

That gave me an idea! Two can play at the same game…

My wife, God rest her soul, knew a little bit about herbs and other plants. She had cultivated certain vegetation for our own private medicinal purposes, and naturally I'd picked up some things from her over the years. Among others, her favourite oleander bush was still growing well in the front garden.

I smiled and chuckled as I added appropriate measures of the concoction to the various foodstuffs. I've convinced myself I'm okay with this plan; he brought it on himself after all, invading my home. I ensured to dose the ice-cream and put it back to refreeze – it would probably be the first thing he'd go for.

I'm so looking forward to getting rid of my intruder, so that I can live my peaceful and happy life again like I had before he arrived.

***

"You're gonna need a bigger boat." – Jaws (1975).

***

MY CHILD MELTS ME: THE GTF

"You definitely can't give sparkling water to a cat!" I say.

"Why not?" asks my brother Flynn. "It would be fun, wouldn't it?"

"Oh really, fun for who, exactly – us or them?" I retort, as the performance continues.

I am Ms Geometry. We have always lived with our extended family: my parents and my grandparents. We have lived off the grid forever, before it was hip to do so. We wash once a week (because it's cold) but we go for dips in the lake. We live by candles after 5.00 pm, but usually go to bed with the chooks. We stomp in a bucket to wash our clothes, and camp out in a tunnel for fun.

With no TV we created the Geometry Theatre Festival (GTF) in our own lounge room. The event started off as simply charades, but now I'm 30 years old, and my parents in their 80s are now grandparents too. We are all raising my children as I was raised, and the GTF has expanded. Today we have a total of 15 actors at large and we put on detailed events. Living as a well-formed tribe, we all know no different. When it's necessary we sort out our disagreements, and we work together as best we can.

These days, would you believe, we take our GTF to what was the local trade market. Our little off-the-grid colonisation members recite narrative poetry and perform song-and-dance numbers.

Hold on to your fabric (that we use as umbrellas) while you dance in the rain, kiddos! There's an old proverb that as a parent I feel is something we all need to carry in our hearts: "Never let your storm get your children wet."

"But *why* can't cats drink fizzy stuff?" my little one persists, after our final comedy skit.

The older kids gesture to their bottoms and make farting noises, while my eldest daughter acts out her best vomiting sequence. We all giggle. My children melt me.

KISSING CHICKENS

I miss you in the morning when the sun shines in. I know we are not done. Behind every romantic story is a reality; I want that reality to be loving and a true fairytale. But how?

The flowers I planted are beginning to bloom, and I sip my coffee and admire them. I have my own life now, and I'm determined to make the most of this beautiful day. But still, I sit a little longer and let my mind wander to far-off lands, and to the time of my childhood…

I daydream of kissing chickens. Memories fill my mind. I would pick up my grandfather's bantam hens, look deep into their eyes, and thank them for their tiny eggs I was about to collect. They would murmur back to me, in their small and simple cluck-cluck way, so softly.

I want to recreate that.

Simple thoughts are the best thoughts.

A CORNER THAT GROWS WEEKLY

I'm a superhero, by script. I'm Lucky Lyn.

I have a dedicated space in my lounge room that I call my 'Superpower Corner'. It's an ornate shelving unit that contains all sorts of treasures, very special to me. There are sea specimens from my many childhood adventures at the beach. There are tiny bits of china I dug up from my grandparents' carrot plot. I even have a collection of weird and wonderful glass bottles that my grandmother's uncle, Tim, acquired over the course of his 76 years. Plus many other little bits and pieces – so many that I stopped counting them long ago.

All of these diverse and fun items are the keepers of my most happy memories. And with each new trinket that I add to the shelves, both my corner and my life grow richer.

Sometimes in the late afternoon the sun catches some of Uncle Tim's glass fancies, and the resulting sparkling rainbows dance across my lounge room wall. Every new sunset creates new patterns, turning the room into a wondrous field where my superpowers frolic and shine bright and spin a different story each time.

In my superpower sparkle, my memories deepen, and I feel more and more alive in the splendour of the mementos that I will ultimately pass on to my family members. It's such a magical feeling to be offering others my superhero sparkle power too.

***

"We accept the love we think we deserve." – The Perks of Being a Wallflower, by Stephen Chbosky (1999).

***

P.S.: I LOVE YOU

"Take a good hard look at yourself," I was told.

Well, self-reflection would be the logical first step to learning how to become a better me. And if I can figure out how to become a better me, that will be good not only for me, but for everyone around me too.

In my childhood, summer used to mean afternoons sitting on the grass watching other people picnic at sunset. In my teenage years, it came with sitting next to a potential boyfriend, with the pit of my stomach lurching and my palms tingling, as I wondered how to hold hands.

Now, in my mid-life years, long hot summers mean something different again. Lonesome nights watching the sunset. Making sure I have all the full-moon dates written in my diary, so that I never miss one.

However, I feel that am still deeply connected to my purpose – I've just forgotten how to enjoy myself.

My rural home was magnificent. But to boost my change, I got away, to an Airbnb city apartment. When I caught my reflection in the entryway mirror, I didn't recognise myself. I examined the owners' photos on the hallway side table. I picked up one of a handsome young man standing next to a canoe. 'Nathan 1983' was noted on the back.

The lights flickered. I went to the fridge, and then left a 'get human food' reminder note for myself under one of the magnets. Fortunately the owners' Airbnb welcome package contained a bottle of Malbec wine and a box of Chickadees snacks ('they're chicken flavoured fun' read the slogan).

I curled up on the couch, under a fluffy blanket, with my food and drink and a book chosen from the well-stocked shelves in the study.

"This will have to do for now," I said out loud. Though in actual fact, it was just what the doctor ordered. I found that I was resetting, relearning, and refinding…bliss.

A colleague had said, "On your next day off, go do something you have never done before."

It wasn't really a postscript, not anymore – reminding myself how to love myself again.

***

"Absorb what is useful. Discard what is not. Add what is uniquely your own." – Bruce Lee.

***

THORA-ROSE

My husband and I had made a good fortune that enabled us to retire in style before we got *too* old. And money was no object anyway once I discovered that we could buy our final and forever home in my old childhood neighborhood, even though things had changed so much in the many intervening years (a huge improvement, some would say).

"I love the townhouse in the CBD! I love the vibe of the city! I NEED that outdoor pool space!" I gushed.

Joseph almost seemed jealous; I think he would have liked to live at 509 Pacific himself. Pity for him that he was only my realtor and not my husband.

Joseph tried to apply some calm to my storm. "You wanted to stay below the ten-million-dollar budget, Thora," he said, gesturing as if on a cable TV commercial.

"No, I want it all now! I want that pool. I want that view. The yard is perfect for Jackson," (who was my actual husband), "and we could get a puppy. Maybe later on, do a few projects… But for now, it's turnkey, and it needs to be mine, as soon as possible."

Joseph was starting to shake his head at the word 'projects' but then he switched to nodding approvingly when he heard 'turnkey'. As I came back to the now, he took my hand as if to propose – I quickly extricated myself, and then to cement my decision (and better occupy his hands before he got even more silly ideas), I handed him a glass of my vintage Krug Champagne. He practically melted into it. After that, he had the rest of his work to do for me.

The purchase was completed, and Jackson and I moved in, and we loved it. The place was beautiful, though big for just the two of us. But it had been just the two of us for so long; we never talked about or even acknowledged the missing third anymore. Those first few days we filled with getting comfortable in our new space, and just starting to talk about all those possible projects in our future.

And then Jackson died. Suddenly, and without any fuss.

We hadn't even chosen our puppy.

I lost my enthusiasm for projects, or for anything, for a long time.

I had shrunk into a void, but then suddenly Ashton came back into my life, after so many years of being estranged from his father, and by extension from me. (Suffice it to say, I'm not necessarily proud of all my past choices.)

For the first time in years, I found some long-lost enthusiasm, and maybe a reason to actually resurrect some projects. Maybe not the same ones Jackson and I would have done, but, something...

I first had a full-sized Appaloosa horse statue fashioned, because that would be special to Ashton. I hoped that Ashton would eventually come and live with me full-time in my beautiful four-story forever home, but I was so far disappointed. I spoke to that horse statue as if it were alive: "Confetti, oh how I love you!" Ashton thought it was very strange that Confetti was 'back', so many years later – it was not long after his sixth birthday that she had fallen ill... He had been inconsolable and his grief had gone on for years. But I secretly witnessed him patting the shiny marble rump and stroking the spotty mane, as if she were real.

More changes followed. It was cathartic, making improvements, getting back into a relationship with my house. My relationship with my son, however, needed its own work.

"Please call me 'Mother' at least, Ashton, and not 'Thora-Rose'," I requested, more than once.

Ashton would reply coolly each time, "Bart Simpson calls his father 'Homer' – good for him, good for me."

Ashton did however love the thought of entertaining his friends and hosting pool parties and referring to this place as his own home in front of them, so that they would think of him as a multi-millionaire. I was not very fond of that idea but was determined that whatever worked to keep him around would be good for me. And he was here a lot, now, while the renovations were ongoing, and there would be opportunities enough for him to show off to his friends when my changes were complete.

One day I was reviewing some plans to remodel the first floor kitchen and dining room. Ashton was there too, watching me with a strange expression on his face.

"Do you know that you are named after a murder victim?" he suddenly blurted out.

I ignored that. "I'm going to build a big glass wall along the pool deck, and out the side of the house to the vine-covered fence. What do you think, Ashton?"

"You even look like her!" Ashton continued, smirking, hoping to rustle my feathers. "Thora Holmquist Rose was born in Sweden in 1920, and she was murdered in Los Angeles in 1963, the year *you* were born. It was a cold case for almost 30 years before some fingerprint evidence resulted in a conviction!"

I was determined not to let him have his way with this sort of macabre talk. "I think a large counter of Italian marble and a new staircase too, some more glass to view this grand space…and hallway mirrors as well, to enhance the natural light."

Ashton was not fooled, or distracted. "What, no curiosity of continuity of a soul or souls?" But he did at least accept that I was not going to humor or bite at his clumsy projection. "Well, just read this, then – *Thora-Rose.*" He held up a thin book with a gray cover. "I'll leave it in the library. I would think you might be interested in these theological writings of what I see as intelligent energies and their journeys after death."

I found the book later where Ashton had left it for me, because he was actually right – I *was* interested in that sort of thing. The book was called 'Awaken From Death' and it contained writings of and about the great Swedish theologian and philosopher, Emanuel Swedenborg.

In time I became quite obsessed with this book; I even wrote my own notes in it. And a shared admiration for the book bridged a gap with Ashton, at last – we discussed its ideas intensely as we finally spoke freely; and we also swam, and drank, and connected at long, long last as mother and son, in my forever house, in my forever home.

When Ashton confided in me about a new girl he was seeing, someone he really, REALLY liked, I had so much hope for his future, my future, our future. He showed me a photo of the two of them together. She was lovely, and the way she was looking at him in the photo gave my heart a little flutter – Jackson had looked at me like that, when we were young... In my mind's eye, I saw Ashton getting engaged, and married – and I saw myself as a doting grandmother. I would have a whole family, and we would all be so happy together. Life would be absolutely blissful. I felt like I had been yearning for such bliss for a very long time. I couldn't wait to meet my son's special girl.

I am happy! I just hope that this connection and these feelings last forever. I think about the ideas in the Swedenborg book. Does forever exist on an infinite level? Maybe so? Oh, how I want it to be so!

***

"We are what we pretend to be, so we must be careful about what we pretend to be." – Kurt Vonnegut.

***

BELOW YOUR FEET

After settling my purchase of Lot 11 and pinning it with flags, every cell in my body was filled with excitement. Gone were the moments where my plans were paused, or even turned to ashes. I was no longer the observer of my own life. Although never immune to all the changes, I felt a euphoric state of accomplishment as I tromped through my very own island dirt.

I had been hooked when I read about the *Portlandia,* a steamship that sank off Maine's Cransten Island in 1885, with the loss of all its passengers and cargo. I felt a calling. I had to get me a piece of the treasure-hunter action.

Now at last the surface investigation of Lot 11 lay ahead of me. My very first excavation efforts revealed a lead-splash musket ball. Next, I turned up a pocket watch (the same as one in an old photo in my hallway back on the mainland). Then, I uncovered a ledger book, done up with a brass buckle and a belt made of 1700s cowhide – it was a ship's log. In it I found inventory pages belonging to an Admiral John Courfresne, dated 1745. I was delighted, and my excitement flared.

In just one day, one dig, finding all these prizes – with this I knew I had created a life for myself on Lot 11, pulling back the veil of my ancient soul purpose.

I returned again and again to my precious soil on Cransten Island. I had yet to find anything that could definitively be said to have come from the *Portlandia,* but that did not diminish my enthusiasm one bit. Even on the days I didn't find anything at all, there was still a promise that perhaps the newest gift would be revealed with the next bite of my shovel. I never gave a thought to building on this land; that was not what it meant to me. The dirt and its secrets consumed me entirely, and I shared them only with my new little dog, Chickadee, who sometimes 'helped' me to dig.

The 12-month anniversary of my Lot 11 purchase saw me back on the island to acknowledge the monumental first moments I had had with my earthen ideal. Under darkening skies I dug in a new place and was rewarded immediately. A tunnel! Lightning flashed and the following thunder persuaded Chickadee to run off, although I called futilely for him to come back. I did know better than to go it alone, and worse, with an approaching storm. But I put the shovel into the dirt again, just once more, to see just a little bit more of that tunnel, before I had to find Chickadee and leave…

Almost simultaneously, the heavens opened and my shovel hit a crucial spot – the tunnel first collapsed underneath me and then caved in on me from all sides. The wild storm fully rolled in, as I was delivered into my earth and became cemented within the embrace of the beloved soil of my Lot 11.

BULLETIN: CRANSTEN ISLAND CLAIMS ANOTHER LIFE

[...]

Ms. Kim Draveen was alone with her puppy, awaiting the untamed storm.

[...]

Ms. Draveen's body has been recovered and released to her family. The family have also taken in Ms. Draveen's dog, which was found alive in the woods.

[...]

The mud of Lot 11 had ultimately yielded up a precious sad prize to the search and rescue recovery workers. But I wouldn't, I *couldn't,* leave my special place.

What shall I do now, though – 11 feet below, on Lot 11?

***

"Do not let the memories of your past limit the potential of your future. There are no limits to what you can achieve on your journey through life, except in your mind."

– Roy T. Bennett.

***

ELEVEN

I'm standing in a hallway. I can see an analogue clock face that tells me it's 11.00.

I look outside. It's dark. Logically that would mean it is 11.00 pm, not 11.00 am. I'm not sure, though, but if so…then what happened to the past 12 hours? Or if it really is still 11.00 am, a storm must be approaching. Or maybe an invisible volcano has blown and the day has turned to night. *No, that's ridiculous!*

I hear a scream upstairs, then nothing. I blink. Trying to figure out what is happening. I feel as though I've woken from a deep sleep, groggy and fatigued. I have no recollection of anything else. I'm a little wobbly on my feet and I have a bruise on the back of my right hand. I listen. *Deep breath in.* I hear my breath.

"Henry!" a woman is screaming. "Henry!" And then there is a second, far-off scream.

It's now light outside. I open the flyscreen door and run onto the porch and down the front steps to the puddles and the muddy ground. I don't recognise anything. I look back at the house. It's a grand old wooden cabin, two levels. No sign of any movement. I get an intense urge to shout out, "Who's there?" Yet in the same second I feel a foreboding, a fear, and a need to run.

The long driveway extends down a hill to the sea. There's an embankment in the other direction and a wooded area, bordered by a well-maintained yard with masses of yellow daffodils dancing in the wind. I see a few outbuildings. The muddy driveway has fresh tyre marks.

I realise I am wearing pants that are too short for my legs (although pleated and well pressed), and a neatly ironed shirt. But no shoes.

I have no idea where I am.

I have no idea *who* I am.

Should I go back inside?

Rain falls suddenly and I find myself standing back in the hallway, looking at a number of framed pictures on the wall and on the dresser there. This time I yell out loud, "HELLO?" There's no reply. "Is anyone home?" I call.

All of the pictures have ornate gold filigree frames. In one there is an elderly lady with a wide-brimmed hat; in another, the same lady and a well-dressed man are wearing their Sunday best and standing outside this house in its heyday. There's also a picture of a small boy and a teenage girl sitting in a red canoe, and one of a family of four all smiling in front of a yeti statue.

I walk into an open floorplan lounge room and kitchen space. Everything is lovely, and new – freshly renovated.

A woman is there, sitting on a barstool. It's the same woman from the family yeti photo. She has her face buried in her hands. There's a pen, and a notepad with a photo taped to it, on the counter in front of her. Behind her on the kitchen wall I notice another clock. It's identical to the one in the hallway, down to also showing 11.00.

"Excuse me," I say, hesitantly, not wanting to startle the woman. "Hello? Um, I'm sorry to bother you…"

There is no reaction from her.

"Excuse me?" I say louder. She continues to ignore me. I feel ill, and afraid, because I know that there is something very wrong here. I think – I hope – that I'm dreaming. I pinch my bruise, and I wince.

No, it's real.

"HELLO! HELLO!" I yell at the woman. And finally she looks up.

"Henry?" she says.

"No…I'm not Henry. Can you help me?" I ask.

The woman looks around and straight past me. I walk right up to her, waving my trembling hands – it seems that she can't see me. I touch her jacket and she flinches, moving her arm away. *What is going on?*

"HELLO?" she says.

"Can you seriously not hear me or see me?" I repeat several times, as I pull on her jacket again. I grab her arm harder than I mean to, and she falls off the barstool and to the floor. I freeze, and watch as she scoots herself backwards across the floor until she's leaning up against the oven door. "Who's there, who are you?" she shouts, her eyes wide as she looks frantically around the room.

"I don't know," I answer, feeling that things are hopeless. "I can't remember anything. But I'm right here!"

I look at the notepad on the counter. The photo taped to it is of a little boy, the same one from the hallway pictures. Underneath it the woman has written a time, and: 'I miss you, Henry.'

I wonder…

I pick up the pen and write something under the time.

The woman's eyes nearly fall out of her head, and she holds her hand over her mouth, looking like she's inwardly screaming. From her position on the floor she can easily see the pen moving 'by itself', firstly as I write, and then as I place the pen down again, on the notepad and photo.

I sit down on the barstool, and wait. For a long time the woman just sits there, silent and frozen to the spot in front of the oven.

Finally she comes to a decision. "Don't touch me, and don't hurt me!" she screams out. "I'm going to look at what you've written." She slowly moves and gets to her feet, making her way cautiously to the kitchen counter. She pulls the notepad closer to her, while still nervously scanning the room. She definitely can't see me – now she's standing directly in front of me, but she clearly doesn't know I'm right there.

I study her face – something else about it is familiar. *Who are you? And what is going on?*

We both stay silent, for a few minutes. Waiting.

She reads my note. "Who are you?" she whispers, speaking the words of my note out loud. "Who are you?" She seems to be talking directly to me, and for a moment I think she can see me, but then I realise she is still just looking straight through me.

"Who am I?" she shakes her head. "Well, I'm Naomi, and I don't know what's going on here." She thinks a moment, and then starts walking around the room, cautiously. She ventures to add, hesitantly, "Henry…is that you?"

Who the damn is this HENRY?

I turn in frustration, and I happen to catch my reflection in the large full-length mirror on the wall next to the dining table and the open fireplace. Almost simultaneously the woman called Naomi walks into the line of the mirror too, behind me, and I freeze and gasp. She steps and turns around and then freezes too, as she looks into the mirror, and she is focussed on my reflection – she is actually LOOKING AT ME.

She and I are now standing side by side, gazing at each other in the mirror. We are equally as tall, and we are dressed identically. We wear the same hairstyle, the same *face,* and the same expression of shock. We inhale at the same time. She is eyeballing me and my eyes are darting to look at her. We both open our mouths to scream…

And then the clock hand moves off 11.00 and everything plunges into darkness. I hear that same scream as before, upstairs, and the sound of a car coming up the driveway, and then nothing. Silence. I feel around, softly, tentatively. In complete darkness. Nothing.

"Hello?" I try. Still nothing. I move my feet now too, and my hands are outstretched, feeling around in the inky blackness for the Naomi woman, but it's obvious she is no longer standing next to me. I move out of the room, and I bang into the dresser in the hallway. One of the framed pictures sounds like it falls, and breaks its glass on the floor.

I hear footsteps coming up the front steps, across the porch, and through the flyscreen door. There are two sets of footsteps, and two male voices. I feel a slight breeze as the two people walk right by me. I'm still feeling around, yet I find nothing, and I see nothing. There's a tinkling of glass as it sounds like someone picks up the fallen photo frame on their way past. I stumblingly follow after the footsteps and voices, back towards the kitchen area.

From by the counter I hear a young boy's voice: "Look, Dad, a message on our notepad!"

"What, Henry?" replies an adult male voice. "REALLY?"

"It worked, it worked!" exclaims the young voice, joyously. "Mum has been here! Look, Dad, it says, *'Meet me here at 11.00. I miss you, Henry'* and then in the same writing but messier, *'I don't know where I am and you can't see me, but I'm here, please just talk, and tell me what's going on?'* Oh Dad, Mum doesn't know she died? This means she is here at eleven?"

Suddenly the room lights up. The kitchen clock hits 11.00 again.

Now there are four copies of me, standing in the kitchen, seeing but not being seen by the man, or by the boy called Henry.

Every one of us four is staring at each of the others as we are all reflected in the mirror. Each one of us holds a bunch of golden daffodils.

DAFFODIL CLOUD

For my father, Keith, who recently turned 90 years old.

This is his favourite poem, 'The Daffodils' (also known as 'I Wandered Lonely as a Cloud'), by William Wordsworth.

This beautiful poem was first published in 1807. It is now in the public domain.

THE DAFFODILS

I wandered lonely as a cloud
That floats on high o'er vales and hills,
When all at once I saw a crowd,
A host, of golden daffodils;
Beside the lake, beneath the trees,
Fluttering and dancing in the breeze.

Continuous as the stars that shine
And twinkle on the milky way,
They stretched in never-ending line
Along the margin of a bay:
Ten thousand saw I at a glance,
Tossing their heads in sprightly dance.

The waves beside them danced; but they
Out-did the sparkling waves in glee:
A poet could not but be gay,
In such a jocund company:

I gazed – and gazed – but little thought
What wealth the show to me had brought:

For oft, when on my couch I lie
In vacant or in pensive mood,
They flash upon that inward eye
Which is the bliss of solitude;
And then my heart with pleasure fills,
And dances with the daffodils.

***

"If one daffodil is worth a thousand pleasures, then one is too few."
– William Wordsworth.

***

Other Publications by Dr. Dee Hacking

SPRUIK IT!: Cultivating the Willingness to Back Yourself to Your Success. Barnes and Noble, 2022. LivingLovingly Press. USA.

The New Rules of Wellness: Transformational Stories from Health Experts Who Lead from the Heart. House of Wellness Publishing, 2023. Australia.

The New Rules of Wellness: Transformational Stories from Health Experts Who Lead from the Heart. Volume 2. House of Wellness Publishing, 2024. Australia.

Change Makers: 21 Transformational Stories from Women Making an Impact in the Lives of Others. Co-author. Change Maker Press, 2020. Australia.

Voices of Impact: Empowering Stories From Female Visionaries and Entrepreneurs. Co-author. Voices of Impact Publishing, 2022. Australia.

A Clue to the Invisible Pyramid. A collection of short stories (Volume 1). House of Wellness Publishing, 2024. Australia.

The Doorway. A collection of short stories (Volume 3). House of Wellness Publishing, 2026 release. Australia.

Eleven. A collection of short stories (Volume 4). House of Wellness Publishing, 2026 release. Australia.

Author's Message and Thanks

Thank you for reading my second volume of short stories! I really enjoyed following up my first short story collection, **A Clue to the Invisible Pyramid**, with MORE new stories. Did you recognise some of the same characters or places across both books? And please be sure to keep looking through the doorway for a new set of adventures, coming soon in my third short story collection!

Thank you to everyone who continues to follow and support me, and to those people who are newly discovering me in their journeys around the internet or with wellness. I love you all and I hope there is something for everyone in my books and/or on my socials.

Once MORE, an enormous thank you to A. W. D. McIntosh (FWC) for editorial assistance, for special collaboration on some stories ('More', 'Snake Tavern', 'The Terra Experiment', and 'Intruder Alert'), and for various additional dialogues and scenario realisations in a number of the other tales. WHAT A TEAM!

Many thanks to UA for my fantastic cover clock and for assistance with photo touch-ups.

To my wonderful husband John, our beloved children and grandchildren, and all our dear family and friends, thank you for your ongoing love and support.

And this one is for my mother, Marie Elson, 1934-2025. She got to hold an advance copy before she passed away, and she said that she could feel how good it was! I am happy that she is now also a part of it – please see page 195.

Once again, thank you to everyone who has come (back) for MORE! It truly means the world to me.

Please connect with me on my socials below to talk about my books, life, the universe…and anything and everything! I would love so much to see you there.

XXXX Dee

Email: houseofwellnesspublishing@gmail.com
Facebook: https://www.facebook.com/nereda.hacking
LinkedIn: Dr. Dee Hacking

Publisher's Message (Get in Touch!)

House of Wellness Publishing is a boutique publisher created and run by Dr. Dee Hacking. Its purpose is spreading true tales of health, wellness and inspiration, along with stories of fiction (including novels and short story collections), and so much MORE!

Dr. Dee originally hails from Melbourne, Australia, but for many years has made her home in the Queensland coastal town of Mackay, where she runs her own highly regarded health clinic (*Bay Massage & Homeopathy Allied Health Clinic - Dr. Dee*) as well as her publishing business.

Dr. Dee is already a bestselling author in the fields of health and wellness, and is delighted to now be publishing her second volume of short fiction with **More**. Stay tuned for the doorway to further delights!

- If it is also your dream to be a published author, perhaps you have something you would like to talk about with Dr. Dee? She would love to hear from you via her socials. Even if you don't think you have something to say **about** wellness, there's a very broad spectrum of subjects and stories that could help **promote** wellness in our readers, so let's have a chat!

House of Wellness Publishing is the originator of the international bestselling **The New Rules of Wellness** (NROW) series. You can find the published NROW volumes on Amazon. ***Author submissions for chapters in our upcoming NROW volumes are currently open (2025-2026)*** – please contact us via the **email** in our socials to discuss.

Socials:
Please see previous page.

A Tribute to My Mother, Marie Elson

In mid-2024, I was delighted to be able to publish **I Choose To Be Happy,** by Marie Elson, my mother. At the age of 89, Marie's dream of seeing her own book published had come true. She was rightfully proud of her achievement, and enjoyed being the 'celebrity author' in her friends group. It was another chapter in her long and full, and of course HAPPY, life. It was also her last great adventure. My beloved mother Marie passed away in July 2025, aged 90. I will miss her forever.

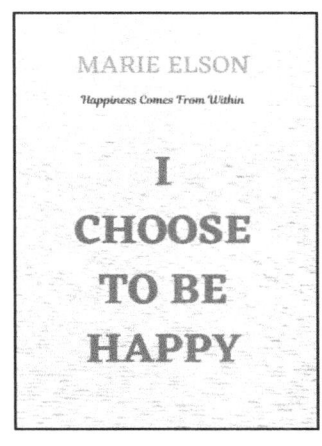

MARIE ELSON

Happiness Comes From Within

I
CHOOSE
TO BE
HAPPY

A happy childhood

Ready to take on the world

Marie was born in December 1934, to parents Robert and Marie McIntosh. She had a happy childhood in country Victoria, Australia, with her parents and younger brother Robert. But as a young adult she wanted to see more of the world, so she did! She travelled around and worked in many countries. She saw the UK, Scandinavia, Russia, and more. She toured around and worked in Canada (at several hotel receptionist positions) and the USA (as a typist for the United Nations in New York) and New Zealand (as a hotel's receptionist AND its hairdresser!). She charmed far-flung relatives and made new friends instantly wherever she went.

Back home in Australia, Marie added to her skills by working at several jobs (sometimes simultaneously), including as a medical receptionist and a ballroom-dancing teacher. She married Keith Elson, and they welcomed me!

Marie with daughter Dee and parents Marie and Robert

Elegance

Over the years Marie also expanded on her love of healing and spirituality by assisting others, and by nurturing this love in me. She always said that I was a natural healer, and I know she was very proud of everything I have achieved and where I am today.

Marie had a lifelong rapport with both people and animals, and she put this to good use for more than 30 years as she became an in-demand housesitter and petsitter. She loved this 'job' passionately (she never really thought of it as 'work') and only gave it up in her late eighties when she retired to a supported community in the seaside town of Rosebud, location of so many happy family holidays over the years. Marie felt a particular connection with nature and was especially a keen and knowledgeable gardener – see **I Choose To Be Happy** for a multitude of her gardening tips and wisdom.

Marie's 90th birthday

Dee and her new grandson Arthur, Marie's great-grandson

In July 2025, Marie had a fall in her garden and was admitted to Rosebud Hospital. There she told the nurses (the wonderful nurses of Walker Ward, who looked after her so well) all about **I Choose To Be Happy**, and how she was busy preparing her next book! Sadly, Marie faded and passed away a week later – peacefully and gently and naturally, as she wanted.

Marie just missed the birth of her great-grandson, but knowing her, I have no doubt that she was there with us in spirit, watching over and taking care of her precious family still.

I have Marie's last writings, and I'm sure that I will include or take inspiration from them in my own future story collections. I will probably smile through tears when I do.

Thank you, Mum, and bless you. Rest in peace. I love you.